TUCKER
VS. THE
APOCALYPSE
A Dystopian SciFi Novella

Jay Allan Storey

Non Sequitur Publishing

Vancouver, BC

December 30, 2024

Jay Allan Storey/Non Sequitur Publishing
566 – 1771 Robson Street
Vancouver, BC V6G 1C9
www.jayallanstorey.com

Publisher's Note: This is a work of fiction. Names, characters, places, and incidents are a product of the author's imagination. Locales and public names are sometimes used for atmospheric purposes. Any resemblance to actual people, living or dead, or to businesses, companies, events, institutions, or locales is completely coincidental.

Website: www.jayallanstorey.com
Email: jayallanstorey@shaw.ca

Book Layout © 2017 BookDesignTemplates.com
Cover by: Kim G Design

- 4 -

Tucker vs. the Apocalypse/ Jay Allan Storey -- 1st ed.
ISBN: 978-1-7776236-9-2

To the hundreds of dogs and other animals who have graced my life over the years. May all that is good be given to them.

Dogs do speak, but only to those who know how to listen.
— ORHAN PAMUK (author, My Name Is Red)

CONTENTS

CHAPTER ONE

THE BEGINING

I see it even now as I stare up at the infinite sky, its deep blue dome shot with endless colours and shades, enveloping the world like the air we breathe, winding its way like a thick scent around every crack and crevice. It emanates from the totality of the world's life forms, both plant and animal, from the tiniest to the largest, each with its own local disturbance swirling, eddying and flowing through the whole.

Long ago, I and all my brothers sensed a change in this aura of the world—this Web of Life. Weak spots were beginning to emerge, threads breaking loose and expanding into holes, slowly tearing the structure apart like a worn-out rag. Something large was coming. Something sinister. But it wasn't until many seasons later that the horror actually began to unfold.

Spring had arrived, and the pink blossoms from the plum tree in our yard were just beginning to float to the ground. I watched the winds blow them swirling down the lane and into the street, as I lay on the window seat in the late afternoon sun. My friend Jerry's car pulled into the driveway as usual, the fallen blossoms swirling in tiny circles around its wheels. When he opened the front door, I leapt from my perch and greeted him as always, wagging my tail, jumping up, and putting my front paws on his waist.

But his own presence in the aura was suddenly weak and sickly; the thread joining him to the Web of Life was stretching and unraveling. His face was pale and covered with splotches, and he was steeped in the overwhelming scent of death. Instead of stopping and playing with me as he usually did, he stumbled up the stairs to his bedroom.

I followed, and took my usual protective spot on the floor at the foot of his bed. As I lay there, his breathing became shallower, and I sensed his aura fading, disconnecting from the great other. I climbed onto the bed and lay beside him, nudging his shoulder, hoping, though somehow I knew it was futile, that the terrible affliction devastating his body would magically recede.

"Tucker," he finally croaked my name.

I nuzzled in closer and licked his face. He made some sounds, as his kind do, but in a whisper, his scent and presence conveying reassurance, regret, sadness, and love. He was saying goodbye. He draped an arm around me. We lay like that until the light began to fade.

Just before dark, his body convulsed, and he expelled a gasp of air. His life-force had detached and faded to nothing, along with those of untold others I could sense in the aura that surrounds us all. The mass of ruptures now exploding through the Web of Life could only mean that countless lives were departing from this world. I sensed an enormous and expanding void in the section of the aura that humanity had once occupied.

Outside, sirens began to scream throughout the neighbourhood, accompanied by the howling, in other houses, of many of my brothers. Sensing the cataclysm that was unfolding, I threw back my head and howled along.

I lay beside Jerry's lifeless body all that night, pressing in closer as panicked shouts and screams echoed in the streets outside and flashing beams of blue and red light projected frightening shadows on the wall. I huddled by his side all the next day, not knowing what else to do. The sirens continued to wail in the distance, concentrated now in the direction of the city nearby.

On the third morning there was silence, and I gingerly rose to my feet. Jerry's motionless body and staring eyes confirmed what I already knew to be true. I studied his face, now frozen in an expression of peaceful rest. During our time together I'd done my best to teach him, and other humans I met, about the Web of Life. I believe all lifeforms, at least all those who are self-aware, can sense its presence—all except humanity. That blindness made it inevitable that their dominance in our world would be temporary, that their kind would eventually fade away and die.

I would miss him, and a few others I had come to know and love. I'd been happy living in this house. Jerry had been my best friend, my protector as well as my charge, and my provider. We had always taken care of each other. I'd never wanted for food or water. Now, I didn't know how I could survive without him.

I left his side, jumped off the bed, and descended the stairs. The already giant rip in the aura was rapidly expanding, swirling above me like a massive black vortex. I stepped into the downstairs hallway and headed for the front door, just as a new set of sirens outside reached a crescendo. The noise was deafening. I ran and hid, shaking, in a closet as several of them screamed by on the street.

Once the wailing had faded into the distance, I made my way to the door, raised a paw and scratched at it. My claws etched a wavy set of lines on its surface, but it didn't move.

I wandered through the silent, empty rooms, hunting for an exit—an open window, a screen with a hole in it, a door left ajar. There was nothing. In the upstairs bathroom a window was open. I climbed onto the toilet seat and from there onto the counter. Standing on my hind legs

I could just reach my front paws onto the bottom of the open window. But even ignoring the deadly drop outside to the ground, now that I was this close it was clear that the opening was too small—I could never squeeze through. This house, that had sheltered and protected me for almost my entire life, had now become my prison.

Back downstairs, I jumped up to my usual spot on the window seat for a glimpse of this new, changed world. I'd no sooner lay down when a speeding vehicle skidded around a corner on the road outside. I leapt to my feet as it clipped the back of Jerry's parked car, then left the pavement, flipped on its side, and smashed into a tree.

It lay there motionless, smoke rising from the hood and one wheel spinning, a man's body slumped forward in the front. A deathly silence followed, broken only by the occasional siren in the distance, and the intermittent howling from houses nearby.

I jumped down and ambled over to my water dish in the corner. I was thirsty but I only took a few tongues' full, understanding that the precious liquid would never be replenished.

CHAPTER TWO

TRAPPED

Even conserving my food and water, I ran out of both within two days. For two more days I lay beside my dish, not knowing what else to do. Eventually, the hunger clawing at my gut and the thirst tearing at my throat drove me to act, and I began a desperate hunt for sustenance.

I followed a strong trail of odours to the kitchen. I was able to pry open the cupboard where Jerry kept my bags of food, and ate until I felt sick. Some of it was moist, and it helped quench my thirst.

A few days later, when my own food ran out, I found a way to haul myself onto the kitchen counter by hooking my claws onto the wooden trim. The cupboards there contained more bags, full of something that smelled like food. I chewed them open, and, over a few more days, devoured all that was there.

I wandered again through the empty rooms, countless layers of scent transporting me back through my time in this place. Every room told a story: Jerry wrestling with me on the carpet in front of the fireplace in the living room, the patch on the floor where I'd peed as a puppy and made him angry, the closet in the hallway that housed the leash and harness I put on when we went for walks.

Fading, but still detectable, was the scent of Melanie, Jerry's girlfriend, ruffing my fur and petting me as I lay on my window seat in the sun, before her aura disappeared uncounted days ago. These shadows, of events and people that would never return, were all that was left.

I made a second pass through the kitchen and finished off any crumbs that had fallen the first time. I even devoured the scraps of some treats I found beside my leash and harness in the closet. The house was now truly empty of food.

Daylight had come and gone many times and I remained trapped. The wailing of the sirens outside continued, but became less and less frequent. The howling of my brothers in other houses, almost continuous since the catastrophe struck, also became sporadic, and was now interlaced with pitiful whimpering. Like me, they were slowly dying.

I thought of Jerry's lifeless body upstairs in his bed, beginning to decompose. If I had to I would do what was necessary, but I knew it would never come to that. The lids on the toilets in both bathrooms were closed. All my attempts to open them had failed, so there was nothing to drink. I sensed that I would die of thirst long before hunger drove me to that desperate act.

The frame of our front door was now shredded from my relentless chewing, in an attempt to escape. Once again I scratched at its already deeply claw-scarred surface hoping to break through, but it was too thick. I jumped up and tried to turn the handle in my teeth, but something was holding the door shut. When I scraped desperately again at the floor, my claws only scratched its hard surface. I was weakening with each passing day. Sometimes I'd find some moisture on the stone floor below the toilet or refrigerator, and lap it up in desperation.

The house was now shrouded in shadowy gloom in the daytime, and completely dark at night. Even the light that had once leaked in from the street was gone. Shaking, I would press closer against Jerry's body, as growling and scraping noises filtered in from outside, and shouts, screams, sirens, and loud bangs echoed in the distance.

One morning, as I made a final desperate pass through the kitchen looking for food, I heard a scratching, shuffling sound from inside the wall, very close to where I was standing. I froze, and soon a group of rats squeezed through a crack beside a nearby cupboard and ventured out, their noses twitching, sniffing warily at the air.

I held my body perfectly still and low to the ground as the group, two adults, three younger ones, and another adult at the rear, crept forward, hunting for scraps. The two at the front looked healthy—probably too fast for me to catch. The three younger ones were too small. It was the one at the back, the slowest, that held my attention. He was plump, trundling along with his head down. I was cloaked in shadow; neither he nor the others noticed me.

I waited until they'd almost passed. The one at the rear was lagging behind. The moment arrived when he was in position. From somewhere deep in my being an overwhelming urge arose—a primordial drive that was ancient and unknowable. It was beyond conscious thought, as if it was infused into the sinews of my body—the urge to attack, to rend, to devastate. It frightened me.

I imagined making the kill—my teeth sinking into the creature's fur and flesh, feeling its bones crack between my jaws, feeling the essence depart from its body and separate from the great other. I'd never killed another animal, but with all the food gone, my life now depended on finding prey and making the kill. Still I hesitated.

Finally, I leapt forward for more than one of my body-lengths, my jaws open wide. I landed, clamping my teeth shut, but they bit on nothing but air. I'd waited too long. The rat was beyond striking distance. It and the others made some panicked noises, scampering away and squeezing through another crack in the wall.

I'd missed my first kill. It would have prolonged my life for a time, but if I couldn't find a way out, I would die. My life-force would become another rip in the aura, joining Melanie, Jerry, many of my brothers in the other houses, and much of humanity. Once again I scratched and clawed everywhere, but there was no escape.

As the days passed, I saw rats and mice a few more times, but was now too weak and slow to catch them. I was deteriorating quickly now, and I could see no way forward. I stumbled upstairs and climbed onto the bed next to Jerry. A swarm of flies now enveloping him lifted off with the shaking of the bed, then settled back down when the danger was past. Even if I was willing to take that final desperate step, Jerry's body was now too badly decayed.

Even with the overwhelming edge of decomposition that now permeated it, his scent comforted me. Darkness began to descend outside, and I was surrounded by a more terrible darkness. I lay down, and closed my eyes, preparing to join him in the great nothingness.

CHAPTER THREE

THE MEN

At daylight I was awakened by a loud bang outside. I struggled to my feet, crawled to the bathroom, and hauled myself up onto the counter. Now desperately weak from hunger and thirst I stretched to the window, put my front paws on the sill, and peered below.

A crowd of men were moving along the street, headed toward our house. Most were staggering and limping and their auras were sickly and fading. Some carried clubs and metal sticks in their hands. As they passed each house a few would break from the group, go to the door, and smash it in. Sometimes there would be shouts, screams, and more loud bangs.

I jumped down and crawled under Jerry's bed—my usual hiding place when something scared me. A while later there were shouts, swirling scents and footsteps on the street outside our house, then on the walk to our doorstep. I whimpered in fear and pressed back against the wall as something heavy smashed on the front door, again and again, until it broke open.

The voices were inside now, shouting, opening and slamming doors, laughing, smashing things. I was shaking as the booming footsteps of a group of men echoed up the stairs. They reached the landing and headed from room to room. Soon there were footsteps outside the door of the bedroom where I was hiding.

A man shouted and made a retching noise as he entered, and suddenly the room was awash with the odour of his stomach contents. A few others entered, gasping and shouting. They circled the bed, ripping apart the furniture, pulling open drawers, smashing things, yelling, ignoring Jerry's body. I was terrified. I tensed, ready to run. One of the men lifted up the blanket covering the bed, and stuck his head down to look.

His face was strewn with festering sores, and his scent was like Jerry's had been as he approached death. I jumped up and bolted for the door. There were shouts and screams behind me. The man from the bed chased me, but he couldn't catch me. I ran down the stairs. There were more men down there, digging through the closets and throwing open all the kitchen drawers. They tried to grab me but I dove through the front door and was gone.

Outside the air was warm. I blinked in the bright sunlight after all that time in the darkened house. In the yard, more men had broken the windows of Jerry's car, and of the wrecked car in the ditch, and were rooting through the interiors. They didn't even notice me. The entrance to the house next door had been smashed in—a body lay across the opening. I ran and ran, my fear overtaking my weakness and exhaustion. I didn't know where I was going, but at least I was free. That freedom infused me with renewed energy.

As I ran, the roads got wider and the small houses were replaced by larger buildings. Wrecked vehicles were scattered over the roadway, some empty, others with bodies slumped at the front, some with bodies elsewhere inside. Some lay overturned in the ditch, still being consumed by smoke and flames. There were also bodies on the ground, all of them human. Many were being torn apart by animals, including some of my brothers.

I passed a few living people staggering along the road. Sometimes dark green vehicles with green-uniformed men, wearing masks over their faces, sped toward me. They raced by, weaving between the wrecks on the road, their sirens blaring and lights flashing. Other uniformed men with metal sticks stood guard behind barriers at some of the intersections, and some larger buildings had people standing guard in front.

Like all the humans I'd encountered since my escape, they smelled of death, and their auras were fading as they unwound from the greater whole. Even at a distance it was clear that the place they occupied in the Web of Life would soon be empty.

I looked up as an ear-splitting whine filled the sky above my head. A gigantic machine with wings like a bird was falling from the sky. I froze—there was no time to run. The scream intensified until it slammed into the earth, embedding itself in the soil of a field not far away.

Dust, rocks and debris flew into the air and rained down around me. A fireball rose from the machine, tearing through its twisted skeleton. I dove into a hollow in the ground and flattened my body, as a wave of searing heat swept over me. The stench of burning oil, plastic, metal, and flesh wafted through the air.

When the heat and smoke had dissipated I climbed out and continued on, the wreckage still smoldering behind me. A ditch at the side of the road had a stream running in it. In places humans had fallen in, their decomposing bodies fouling the water. It took some time, but I found a clean stretch, and drank my fill. Slowly I began to come back to life.

I looked up again as a huge flock of crows blackened the sky over my head, squawking and flying in the direction of a large structure in the distance. They were soon joined by other birds, all converging on that spot. That could only mean one thing—food.

I took off after them, and soon stood in front of a huge building at the center of an open space dotted with cars. The glass blocking the front had been smashed and some humans were staggering away from the gaping hole, their arms full of packages. Desperate for sustenance, I skirted widely around them and ventured inside.

Along with the crows, many other birds, cats, rats, squirrels, raccoons, some of my brothers, and wild animals I didn't recognize, wandered or flew up and down the aisles, grabbing food from shelves or pecking, licking, or chewing it on the floor. There were a few humans as well, but they too were preoccupied with the food, and were easy to avoid.

Most of the shelves were empty. Both animals and humans were fighting over what was left. I reached an open aisle and stumbled on a huge muscular dog and a small one tugging on either end of a large bag. The big dog finally let go of its end, lunged forward, and grabbed the little dog in its teeth. The poor little one yelped as the attacker clamped its jaws shut and shook it, tearing its tiny body in half. The big one sat consuming its kill and ignored me.

I ran to the next aisle. A group of crows had converged on something on the floor. They flapped up as I approached, and I rushed in to get some of what they'd been eating. It turned out that they were feasting on what was left of a man in a black suit. There was still other food around, so I left it to them.

I rushed toward a far corner where dogs, cats, and raccoons were swarming around a counter, surrounded by the scent of meat. Glass blocked the front, but its back was open, with packages of meat inside. From the scent it was clear that the meat was already turning, but many were eating it anyway. The few remaining humans in the store didn't seem interested.

I backed up, gathered all my strength, ran forward, and leapt onto the counter, then down to the back to join the others fighting for a bite. I traced the scent of an unspoiled package to the middle of the top shelf.

Climbing on the backs of the heaving crowd and springing for the shelf, I pounced on the package, just as a giant black and brown coloured dog did the same. He turned on me, and was about to rip into my throat when several other dogs dove in, distracting him. A massive fight ensued. In the confusion I was able to tear off a large chunk of the meat and swallow it. It tasted bad, but I hoped I could keep it down.

I jumped back to the floor and wandered the aisles like the others, frantically searching. Very soon there would be nothing left. In one aisle, a man was fighting with a dog over a bag of cookies. As the two collapsed onto the floor, wrestling, the bag broke, and the contents spilled everywhere. I snuck in, gulped down as many as I could, and took off.

I cruised the aisles, scavenging, until I was full. Though my thirst and hunger were satisfied and my strength was gradually returning, I was still weak and exhausted. I needed a safe place to hide and recuperate. I passed back through the shattered wall, and across the wide expanse in front of the building. A few of the humans who had been carrying out arms full of food when I arrived now lay on the ground dead or dying, their plunder strewn around them. I found an unopened bag with a picture of cookies on it, grabbed it in my teeth, and took off.

CHAPTER FOUR

OUTSIDE

I was afraid to return to our house, or any of the houses in our neighbourhood, in case I met up with the gangs of men. I still had the bag of cookies in my teeth. I dug a hole on a nearby hill and buried it. I could come back for it later.

It was still morning. I turned toward the rising sun. In the distance lay the city, and the building where Jerry used to go every day. He had taken me with him a few times, and his scent would still be there. After all that had happened, I longed for a place that was comforting and familiar. I headed down the hill toward a distant cluster of shapes projecting like massive blocks from the earth, the early rays of sunlight glinting from their glass exteriors.

By the time I arrived on the outskirts the sun was lowering in the sky. I entered a vast open space. Monstrous square facades loomed above me as I walked, their lengthening shadows breaking the grey of the street ahead.

Animals had already begun to invade the city. I soon joined a host of dogs, cats, raccoons, coyotes, rats, and many others I didn't recognize, streaming toward its heart, somehow aware of the sudden absence of humanity. They slunk between the wrecked vehicles, climbed up the walls, or scurried back and forth along the empty streets and sidewalks, hunting for food.

A shard of glass smashed to the ground at my feet, and I looked up. The top of the building beside me was stained black, wisps of smoke twisting from its roof. The glass at the top had shattered, and flocks of crows, pigeons, and predatory birds now flew in and out of the opening. I moved away from the nearest walls, always watchful.

When I'd visited before with Jerry the roar of vehicle engines, honking of horns, and wailing of sirens had been constant, deafening and frightening. Now, apart from the sirens, which were becoming less and less frequent, the only sounds were the calls of the birds and the howling and grunting of animals.

I skulked through the silent streets and alleys, scanning every shadow. The black mouths of countless hidden nooks and alcoves crouched beneath and between the monoliths crowding around me. Danger and death might be lurking in any one of them.

Flames had engulfed some buildings, and thick black smoke rose high into the sky. Abandoned vehicles were scattered everywhere, some parked on either side of the street, some stopped in the middle, some crashed into buildings, or each other. Many had the bodies of humans inside. Some were black and smoldering, and flames still licked around the skeletons of others. I could feel the heat and smell the death and devastation.

Sometimes I was forced to dive out of the way as a green or white vehicle appeared and raced between the wrecks, siren blaring and red lights flashing. I also saw more people in green or white uniforms. There were much fewer than before, and their auras were even more sickly and thin. A few times I saw people in white carry someone toward a white vehicle.

I pressed into the shadows as a gang, like the one that had smashed down our door, but much larger, swaggered past. Like the others, they carried clubs and metal sticks in their hands, and were smashing in the doors of buildings and carrying away whatever they found. Once or twice I spotted lone humans stumbling around in a daze. All those I saw were clearly sick, and probably dying.

I followed the scent landmarks I remembered from previous visits. My step quickened and I felt a wave of relief when Jerry's building came in sight. Jerry's decaying body still lay on the bed in our house, but I longed to experience his untainted scent again, even for a short time. Maybe here everything would be the way it was, back before all of this... And Jerry might have friends here who were still alive. I might be able to detect his scent on them, and they might help me.

I'd almost reached the building's entrance when a low growl echoed from a dark hollow just ahead of me. I sniffed the air, and the fur at the back of my neck rose. Even before they appeared, the host of scents, screaming despair and starvation, warned me what was coming. One of my brothers, snarling and hungry, his skin stretched tight over protruding ribs, slunk out from the blackness. He was followed by another from the top of a large green bin, and another out of the open window of a wrecked car, until I was facing a full pack, poised to strike.

The Alpha, a huge black and brown monster, approached. The muscles of his chest rippled as he moved. His hackles were raised, and his lips pulled back to reveal a deadly set of fangs. I glanced over at Jerry's building in the distance, thinking back to other times I'd been there. It offered no escape routes, and anyway, it was too far away.

I scanned the square around me. A massive truck was embedded in a nearby wall, a human body slumped in the front. The crash had opened a crevice just above the ground, and through it I could see the pavement of another alley. The wall was too high to climb. I was sure I could fit through the crevice, and I was pretty sure the big Alpha couldn't.

But first I would have to fight my way past the slavering pack that stood in my path.

I backed away, circling toward the wall, keeping the crevice in sight. The Alpha pawed the ground and let out a low growl as he crept toward me, preparing to strike. The others held back, waiting to see what the leader would do. I continued backing toward my escape route, my eyes fixed on the Alpha's form, watching for the flexing neck and shoulder muscles that would tell me it was time to run.

Suddenly, I got that signal, and his claws tore at the pavement as he exploded toward me. I turned and raced for the opening. It was unlikely I'd reach it in time, but I hoped I could get within jumping distance and somehow fend my attacker off.

He leapt into the air and landed on my back, trying to clamp his open jaws around my throat. I twisted my body and rolled out from under him, then head-butted his shoulder, turning him sideways. He yelped as I sunk my teeth into his hind leg.

As he curled his body back trying to reach me, the others charged forward, growling and barking, blood lust in their eyes. I had worked my way to within a single body-length of the crevice. I took a chance, let go, and dove towards it. The Alpha dog turned and again pounded after me, his jaws opened wide, but with the injury to his leg, he couldn't catch up.

I reached the crevice and squeezed through, the Alpha snapping at my heels. On the other side, I felt myself falling. I landed unhurt on the pavement of the new alley, which passed behind Jerry's building. The Alpha tried to follow me, but as I'd guessed, his body was too big to fit. He shoved his head through the crevice and snapped at me in frustration, drool dripping from his fangs.

I took off down the alley, glancing back to check on my pursuers. After several tries, the Alpha finally grasped that he couldn't fit through and backed away, allowing some of the other dogs access. I flew around a corner, just as one of them squeezed through the opening and jumped to the street. I turned another corner, and the front of Jerry's building came into view. The barking of numerous dogs now echoed off the walls of the alley behind me.

Panting heavily, I reached the entrance, and bounded up the stairs to the shattered glass of the building's doors. Picking my way through the shards covering the floor, I entered a huge open space, and pressed my body against the closest wall. The barking and yelping of the pack echoed past the opening and continued down the street, gradually fading into the distance.

I was safe—for now.

I could detect a faint remnant of Jerry's scent, and followed it across the space to a massive pair of metal stairways. I remembered them from times I'd visited with Jerry before. Back then they'd been moving, their menacing hum reverberating through the air, their metal jaws grinding together, threatening to devour me. Jerry had eventually convinced me to jump onto them, and I had stood shaking as they carried us upward to the next floor.

Now, they were still.

I gingerly stepped onto the first step, its surface cool under my foot. It didn't move. Satisfied that the monster was really dead, I followed the scent up and eventually the familiar smells told me that I'd reached Jerry's floor. The odour of death and decay hung like a mournful cloud all around as I padded down a long, silent hallway.

At its far end another door was smashed, and glass was scattered on the floor around it. A knot of crows flapped into the air as I entered a massive room with a series of low walls crowded with desks and chairs.

Bodies were scattered among the chairs and aisles, some partly consumed. Most of the machines that had sat on the desks when I visited before were gone. Some were completely missing, others lay smashed to pieces on the floor. Somewhere in the vast ocean of scents I recognized Jerry's. I followed it to a distant corner, and to a familiar desk and office chair.

I raised my head and sniffed at the air. Images spun into my head as I inhaled the countless scents, old and new, that lingered in the room. I recognized the overweight lady who wore flowery dresses, and who used to fawn over me and give me treats whenever I visited, and Granger, Jerry's friend, who sat at a desk across the room.

The layers of scents from the distant past brought up images of re-animated humans, strolling back and forth between the walled spaces, talking, laughing, holding food in their hands, sitting at the desks, tapping on their machines, and making marks on paper, as they loved to do.

More recently came the anxious sweats of a vastly reduced number, sensing that something was wrong, but with no idea what it was. Later still, the numbers fell even more steeply, and the scents altered, the component of fear intensifying. Finally, there was the sharp tang of terror—the tiny fraction of remaining scents descending into mindless panic.

Deep in the background, interwoven with all the other scents, I detected the odour of food. Hunger now overruled my fear as I followed my nose, padding through a maze of hallways, toward what smelled like a non-putrefied food source. Along the way there were more bodies. The smell of food was overwhelming as I entered an expansive room full of tables, chairs, and machines.

A cluster of crows burst into the air as I arrived, flapping around the room and screeching. I jumped back as I spotted what they had been feasting on—the remains of a middle-aged woman in a colourful, flowery dress. I chased the crows away, and almost got my teeth around the leg of the closest one. What was left of my former benefactor still sat on a chair, her torso draped over one of the tables. There were a few other bodies, sitting in chairs, or lying on the floor.

Too hungry to dwell on my shock or sadness, I turned my attention to the source of the food scent I'd detected. It was wafting from a set of cupboards on the wall above a counter. Eventually the crows decided it was safe to ignore me and settled back down to their meals, along with the rats, raccoons, and other animals that scuffled through the room.

I jumped up on a chair, climbed onto the counter, and was able to nudge one of the doors open with my snout. Inside were square bags with pictures of some kind of thinly layered food. I dragged one out onto the counter, and tore it open with my teeth. I managed to gobble almost all of it down before the crows arrived looking for their share, angrily shrieking around me.

In a nearby room, beyond another smashed door, there were toilets, some with the tops open. I rested my paws on the edge of one and drank my fill. The cupboard door where I'd gotten the food had closed after I hauled out the first bag, so the remaining bags would be safe. I had a guaranteed food source—for a while.

The light outside the windows was fading as I wandered back to Jerry's chair, climbed into it, and lay down to sleep, comforted by my full stomach and his familiar, lingering scent.

CHAPTER FIVE

THE CITY

With nowhere else to go, I stayed at Jerry's building for several days. His desk and chair were against the wall in a corner of the room, where I could keep watch for approaching danger. There was always water to drink from the open toilets, and there were no bodies nearby, nothing to attract the scavengers.

When the bags of food ran out, I began to leave the building by day and run through the corpse-strewn streets. I kept an eye out for my original attackers, but they must have moved on and found another hunting ground.

For a while I scrounged for scraps in buildings lining the streets, many of which had their front windows smashed. When those were cleaned out, I switched to pushed over plastic bins and big metal containers.

One night I was about to re-enter Jerry's building after a scavenging run when a gang, bigger than any I'd seen before, approached on the street. I pressed into a shadowed alcove as a much smaller group appeared, dressed in green uniforms and carrying metal sticks. They blocked the gang's progress. The two groups began shouting at each other and gesturing angrily.

Confident at first, the uniforms began to back up as the gang resumed their march. I crawled deeper into the shadows. Suddenly there was a torrent of screams and loud bangs as the gang charged forward, took the uniforms' metal sticks, and slaughtered them all. The gang then moved on as if nothing had happened.

I decided to search for a new hiding place. Jerry's scent was fading, and the stench of death and decay inside was quickly overpowering it. In an alley a few blocks from Jerry's building, a vehicle had smashed into a wall and was standing almost vertically, with its front window shattered. By walking along a ledge formed by what was left of the wall, I could climb onto its fender and through the opening, and sleep on one of the chairs inside. There were no bodies, so it smelled better. And it gave me easier access to the outside sources of food—the only ones I could find now.

What was left of most of the human bodies in the city had begun to turn. In the past few days, in some of the open spaces, I'd seen huge stacks of them on fire, adding to the stench that now permeated every corner. On rare occasions I would still see a live person. There were bound to be fresh bodies available, but I had no idea where they were. As hungry as I was, I still wasn't ready to follow that path.

As I dug through the piles of garbage looking for scraps, I would often have to fight off competitors, including some of my brothers. Sometimes I would spot a pack, like the one I'd encountered when I first arrived, but now I was more wary, and was able to avoid them.

One day, a tiny dog with a pointed snout and long, matted fur showed up at the dump where I was foraging. I snarled and bared my teeth, and he backed off. But he looked so pitiful and thin, I gave in and allowed him to join me.

He followed me back to my new hiding place and we continued to forage together. I called him Furball. It was good to have a companion.

It helped ease the loneliness I'd felt since Jerry's death. We soon became friends.

One morning we were sifting through a garbage pile when Furball pulled out a short length of rope. He held it in his teeth and play-bowed, daring me to take it. I chased after him, and we continued on until the sun was sinking low, running, jumping, playing tug-of-war, stealing and re-stealing the prize. At night, we would huddle together in my hiding place, comforting each other as sirens, screams, and explosions sometimes still echoed through the streets.

But every day the piles were more and more picked over, and the battle for what was left got more desperate. And now I had to fight off other animals not only for my own share, but for Furball's as well. One day, as we dug through a pile we'd both worked before, a gigantic dog with a muscular chest and huge head showed up.

We both stood our ground, snarled at him, and tried to frighten him off. His ribs were showing, but he was still more than a match for either of us. He charged, driving us away, and began digging through the pile himself. We hung around the edge of the square, hoping he'd give up and go elsewhere.

He growled and whimpered as he dug frantically through the pile, which contained almost nothing edible. Occasionally he would glance in our direction. Sensing danger, I began to back away, and little Furball followed me. Finally the big dog stopped his digging and turned our way, his eyes mad with hunger. We had waited too long. I turned and started to run. With his tiny legs, Furball had a hard time keeping up.

Reluctantly, I stopped and waited, as the huge dog pounded toward us. When Furball caught up I took off again, but our pursuer soon overtook us. When he snapped at Furball I jumped into his path, snarling and baring my fangs. He lunged at me, forcing me to dive out of the way. The monster flew past me and clamped his jaws around Furball, who yelped and writhed in his grip. I leapt onto the attacker's back, and sunk my teeth into his neck.

With an explosive lurch, he threw me off, and I landed in a heap on top of a pile of debris. He continued to shake Furball in his enormous jaws. I heard a snap, and suddenly my friend was limp and silent. The big dog dropped the now lifeless body and approached me. There was nothing more I could do—I ran for my own life. I was much faster, and soon left him far behind.

Gangs, smaller but more dangerous, continued to prowl the streets, and the larger animals were becoming more and more desperate. Even the men in the green and white uniforms had disappeared, and now the swarms of flies and the stench of burning corpses were everywhere, choking off whatever life remained in the rising heat.

The next day I left the city. I climbed a nearby hill and gazed down at the devastation. All was quiet now, with only the chirping of birds and growling of animals occasionally breaking the silence. Hovering over the skyline was a terrifying rent in the aura, like a swirling spiral cloud. The darkness pushed outward and down on me like a smothering blanket. The stench of death flowed out of the place, washing over everything in its path.

I turned and ran, ran until I was exhausted. I found another hill with a view of the surrounding country below and lay down in a protecting clump of bushes to sleep, nightmares of death and devastation surging through my mind.

CHAPTER SIX

FLEEING

The next morning, still frightened and confused, but yearning for a connection to my past life, I returned to the main road, and headed for the familiar winding streets and comforting houses of the block where I used to live.

On the way, I dug up the bag I'd buried earlier, and ate everything in it. Below me was the building I and the others had raided for food when I first escaped. It now stood empty and silent, the broken windows and bodies in front the only reminders of what had once taken place there.

The scent-trail on the path I was following told of ever-expanding death. With every step there were more bodies, either dead from sickness, or torn apart by the men that had been roaming the streets.

As I approached our block, a crowd of those men appeared in the distance. There were fewer than before, but their behaviour was more aggressive, and they still carried the clubs and metal sticks in their hands.

One of them pointed at me, and a smaller group broke away and headed in my direction. I ran, and they quickly gave up the chase and rejoined the others. The scents that wafted to me on the light breeze foretold that they too would be dead soon. Until then they were still dangerous.

I climbed another hill with a view of Jerry's house for one last look, and to say my final goodbye. Down below, not far away, a new gang of men were marching in my direction. I turned and headed for the trees.

On my way, I made a detour to the dog park where Jerry and I had spent so many hours. As I'd expected, it was empty of both dogs and people. But as I'd hoped, I could still detect traces of Jerry's scent, as well as my own, and I stood in the center, sniffing the air, reveling in the memories. I explored the profusion of scents around me. The most recent ones brought back a memory:

I jumped up and down, barking excitedly and wagging my tail, ready for the next run.

"Ready Tucker? Ready?" Jerry said, his smile widening as he swept his arm back, holding the ball in his hand.

I watched intently as he hesitated for a moment, then faked a throw, teasing, before finally whipping his arm forward and letting go. I rocketed across the field, my gaze locked on the tiny round object arcing far above my head. It landed a few body lengths away from my position, and bounced high in the air. I was right under it. I jumped up, grabbed it in my teeth, then flew back and delivered my prize.

I closed my eyes for a moment as I thought of Jerry. Once again the sadness overwhelmed me.

One of the scents was stronger, more recent, than the others. I put my nose to the ground and followed it, and it grew in strength as I approached a small bush on the far side of the green lawn. The bush shook as I arrived. I poked my head around. A dog about a quarter my size, with a flattened face and long yellow and brown fur, jumped out from under it, barking furiously at me. I recognized him—it was Rudy, the little dog from the house next door.

He was shaking, with terror in his eyes, and a bloody scar on the side of his face. Like me, he was still wearing his collar. I'd met him a few times before on walks with Jerry, and we'd played here in the park, in happier days. I took a step toward him. He cowered, barked even louder, and jumped back. I stood for a moment, letting him process my scent and body language. Finally, he relaxed a little as he recognized me. We greeted and sniffed each other. His scent was a deluge of hardship, pain, and desperation.

The dog park stood on the outskirts of town. Rudy followed as I made my way up to a wide road that headed out of the city. There was nothing left for us here. The expansive roadway allowed us to see far ahead, to avoid any dangers that might be approaching. The stench of decay and death faded as the road led us into the wilderness, snaking up toward the mountains in the distance.

In the past, it would have been crowded with all kinds of vehicles, big and small, traveling at such speeds it would be almost impossible for us to dive out of the way. Now the endless expanse of pavement was silent as we walked along the shoulder.

A few wrecks were scattered there, or stopped in the middle. Others had driven completely off the road and crashed into the forest. Some had left the surrounding trees black and burnt, and the shells of a few continued to smolder. Sometimes we would see a human body lying near an empty one, but most of them had the doors closed, with bodies inside.

The sun was still high in the sky when the air came alive with unusual scents from somewhere in the distance. We headed to the edge and looked over. In a small valley stretching below, several cow carcasses lay within an area surrounded by a metal fence. Thick green pasture blanketed the ground outside the fence, but inside, between the carcasses, was nothing but torn up dirt. From their scents, it was clear that the carcasses could be something to eat.

We made our way down. I'd planned to look for a spot to dig my way under the fence, but on arrival we saw that something had already dug a way in, big enough for us, but too small for a cow.

We squeezed through it and into the pen, approached the nearest carcass, and sniffed at it. Though it was beginning to turn, and was skin and bones, there should be parts that were edible. I chose a spot at the back, near the tail, that looked like it had meat on it, and tried to bite through the skin. It was a lot harder than I was expecting. I tried again on the shoulder, but there was no way I could get through the thick black fur and tough hide.

Rudy was having even more trouble. The shape of his face and jaw made it impossible for him to penetrate the skin of the animal. I glanced over at him, trying to sink his teeth into the carcass, then trotting around it, his stubby legs working double time. Finally he stopped and stood barking at it, as if that would help.

Eventually giving up on the shoulder, I moved down to the belly. It was much softer, and the skin seemed thinner. It took a lot of bites, but I was able to tear it apart and get at the meat underneath. Rudy shoved his head in, and we both grabbed as much as we could.

There would be a lot of meat on a cow, even these skinny ones. The carcasses could provide ample food for days. I was considering whether to stay in this place, when I heard a low, frightening growl behind us. Rudy and I both turned to look.

A huge animal with coarse, grey-black fur, a long snout, and pointed ears, crouched a few body-lengths away, its lips curled back to reveal glistening fangs. Behind it were several others, all poised to strike. I'd seen and smelled one running through the streets of our neighbourhood long ago, before some men came in a vehicle and hauled it away—these were wolves, the wild version of my brothers.

For a moment I froze. Rudy dove between my legs and took off across the pen before I even had a chance to move. I finally snapped out of my stupor and flew off after him, squeezing back through the hole in the fence. I glanced behind me as I ran. The wolves' heads were down, feasting on the animal I had opened up for them. They wanted the meat of the cows, not us. We abandoned the field and headed back up the hill to the road above.

We walked, moving continually uphill, until the sun was low in the sky. Sometimes one of us would pick up the scent of food in one of the vehicles, but usually there was no way in. Eventually, we came across one with a door lifted at the back, and the overpowering odour of meat wafting from the opening. As we got closer, we could see the body of a man lying on the road beside the open door. Several rats scurried away as we approached.

There was no movement or sign of life in the shadowed interior. Hunger was quickly overtaking our fear of what might be lurking inside. The scent emanated from a container resting on a pile of boxes in the center. Though the food was turning, at the moment it was our only choice.

A swarm of flies lifted off as I sniffed the body on the ground. It was decaying, and partly eaten by the rats. I had to step over it to jump into the back. I climbed up on the pile of boxes and chewed on the top of the container. Nothing happened, it wouldn't open. Rudy barked encouragement as I pushed it over and stepped on it.

I yelped as it rolled off the pile, bounced on the floor of the vehicle and popped open. The scent of meat was overpowering as a wrapped package tumbled out. I grabbed it in my teeth, leapt back down, and ran from there, with Rudy close behind. Safely hidden in some brush, we feasted on our prize—white, chewy squares with meat inside. Along with what we'd eaten of the cow, it was enough to keep us going for another day.

The light was beginning to fade. Our bellies stuffed, we found a den-like cavity high on a hill and lay down, ready to sleep. I looked over at Rudy. Faced with the wolves, while I stood there frozen, waiting to be their dinner, he'd been smart enough to run for his life.

The next morning Rudy and I continued on, walking along the roadway. I had no idea where we were going. I just wanted to escape the violence and death of the city. Out here in the wilderness the air was fresh and clean. The sky was empty of clouds, and the light breeze in our faces was warm. We'd found a few puddles and streams along the way, but we hadn't eaten since the car with the open door. We were finding fewer and fewer vehicles on the road, and none of those with the scent of food were accessible. We left the road, and followed a rough trail into the trees.

I'd chased a few birds and squirrels before, when Jerry let me off my leash, but I'd never managed to catch any. Back then I'd done it more for fun than anything, knowing I could always get a meal at home. Out here, we were going to have to fend for ourselves. I'd missed the rat in Jerry's house, my first chance to make a kill. In the forest there should be prey. We'd just have to learn to catch it.

We made our way along the trail, scanning for prey as we moved. The sun was high in the sky when, unexpectedly, we caught the scent of cooking flesh. Cooking meant fire, fire meant humans, and in this new, frightening world, humans meant danger. But Jerry and others I'd met had always been generous with their food—and we were getting hungry.

The scent led us to a small glade in the forest, and we crouched in the surrounding brush. A group of ragged-looking men were roasting a large carcass over a fire, the smoke twisting into the air, carrying the scent of a type of meat I didn't recognize. Their auras showed the same sickness we'd seen in all the others. We hung back, hoping for a chance to grab an unguarded remnant. The men grunted and slurped, wiping their arms across their mouths as they tore the flesh from large shanks of meat in their hands.

One of them glanced up and spotted me. I jumped back, expecting an attack, but he smiled and held up the piece of meat in his hand. The scent was almost irresistible. The juices began to flow around my tongue. I edged forward, with Rudy close behind me. The group stopped eating and were all watching us. There was an uneasy silence. They were smiling, but their body language was off. One of the men at the back reached for something.

I glanced at an object lying in the grass at the edge of the clearing. What I saw in the shadows was unmistakable—the drooping ears and long pointed snout, the lolling tongue and large teeth. It was the severed head of one of my brothers.

I yelped and took off, with Rudy close at my heels. There were several loud bangs, and the dirt beside me exploded into the air. A few of the group ran after us, but eventually gave up. Soon we were deep into the forest and at a safe distance.

CHAPTER SEVEN

A NEW FRIEND

A light drizzle began to fall as we continued along a trail through the woods. The incident with the men, as frightening as it had been, had also reminded us how hungry we were. I was shaking off the rain when the bushes on one side of the trail in front of us began to rustle. The glossy leaves of a nearby plant parted and a pigeon-like bird appeared, pecking at the ground. I froze in place, and glanced back at Rudy. He was also stopped in his tracks.

The bird was intent on the seeds at its feet, and so far hadn't noticed us. I moved one foot forward, then another, slowly edging my way closer, hardly daring to breathe. I'd never had to hunt before, but somehow I knew how to move, though I wasn't exactly sure what I would do if I caught my prey.

Finally I was within striking distance. I was about to pounce when a stick beneath my right foot cracked. The bird looked up, noticed me, squawked, and flew away. Later, Rudy and I tried to corner a squirrel, but it ran up a tree.

The drizzle finally stopped as we took a fork in the trail that led deeper into the bush. Above us, through the tops of the towering trees, the sun moved across the sky as we walked on, still hungry. The day was almost over, and we had yet to find any food.

Rudy suddenly veered off, intently sniffing at the ground. He circled around a spot in the weeds and began digging. I joined him, and in a short time we'd uncovered some kind of root that looked and smelled like it might be good to eat.

Too hungry to care whether it was safe, we gorged ourselves on the roots. By the time we'd finished, it was starting to get dark. We took shelter under some bushes on a nearby hill, and fell asleep. Thanks to Rudy we would live for another day.

When I woke, the light was just beginning to rise. I made my way to an open spot at the top of the hill. I could still see the city far in the distance below. There had been a few lights the night before. Now they had all disappeared, and the cluster of block-like buildings gradually emerged from the shadows in the rising light. All was silent. The rent in the aura was now gigantic—a black well of emptiness where an ocean of human life force had once dominated. Almost all traces of humanity had disappeared.

Every day the aura was transforming—the patchwork of holes coalescing to form one gigantic void. Giant swirls of colour now flowed like oil around the newly opened space, expanding, contracting, stretching out, compressing, curling, spinning away in interlacing spirals.

The component humanity had once occupied was quickly being replaced by the auras of countless other lifeforms: plants, trees, mammals, reptiles, birds, fish, insects, that were now flourishing without the carnage inflicted by humanity. Life was irrepressible after all. The world would continue—just in a wildly different form.

Rudy soon joined me. We sat for a while watching the city below, then headed out, first returning to the spot where we'd eaten the roots before. There were still some remnants left, and we might not find any more food for a while. As we approached, I caught the scent of one of my brothers, and we heard the rustling of leaves.

We raced to our root cache, and found a mid-sized dog with floppy ears and a bushy tail hovering over it. His long snout was buried in the dirt, chewing on what was left of our find. He looked a lot like me, but instead of the brown and black of my fur, his shaggy coat was a solid light grey.

Rudy and I rushed forward, snarling and baring our teeth. The grey dog turned, growling at us, blocking our access to the cache. I leapt toward him, barking and snapping, ready to fight. We sparred, but he soon stopped and assumed a submissive posture, his ears flattened against his head, his tail lowered. Like Rudy and me, he was wearing a collar. His scent and body language no longer showed aggression.

Rudy continued to yap behind me as I moved up to meet the stranger, and we sniffed and greeted each other. Rudy eventually relented, and pawed at the ground in triumph, then joined us. The dog was trying to fend for himself, as we were. Before the catastrophe, I had seen him in the neighbourhood, walking on a leash with his companion.

I was reluctant to share our root find, but his fur was matted and lackluster. It looked like he hadn't eaten in a while, and I knew what it was like to be starving. I stood aside. Rudy let out one last low growl, but also stepped away. At first the newcomer hesitated, but his hunger finally overcame his fear. He moved forward and once again attacked what was left of the roots ravenously.

For a time, Rudy and I watched him devouring the remnants of our cache. Even the day before there hadn't been much left. We decided we'd shared enough. When we moved in to join him, he turned and snarled at us. I snarled back, defiantly. He finally moved aside and allowed us in.

Soon there was nothing left under our noses but dirt. Rudy and I turned to leave, and we allowed the new arrival, who I decided to call Greyback, to join us as we continued on our way along the trail. The roots helped stave off the worst of our hunger, but they weren't enough. We needed meat, and we needed it soon.

The trail opened onto an expansive field. As we walked, I caught the scent of an animal somewhere in the tall grass. I stopped and held perfectly still. The others froze behind me. Soon I heard a rustling sound in the direction of the scent. Watching closely, I noticed the branches move in a nearby bush, and beneath it, saw a small brown shape rooting through the grass.

I'd seen them before on walks with Jerry: light brown, with tiny ears, big bulging eyes, puffy cheeks, and a short stubby tail—a gopher. I crouched down and slunk toward it, approaching slowly, as before. The animal still hadn't noticed me.

Finally within attack distance, I tensed my back legs, ready to pounce. The little gopher sat unknowing, its nose twitching as it occasionally looked up from its feeding and sniffed the air.

I leapt forward, my mouth opened wide and teeth bared. I clamped my jaws shut, certain that I'd caught my dinner, but got a mouthful of dirt. I spit it out, and shook my head, confused. The creature's scent told me that it had run into a small hole in the ground nearby. Rudy and Greyback joined me trying to dig it out.

Working together, the three of us soon opened a hole twice as wide as my body-length, and half as deep. But the gopher's passage continued deeper, and there was no sign of the animal. After a bit more digging we gave up. It had escaped. Hunting wasn't going to be as easy as I'd hoped.

Later that day, the tan, pointed tips of a pair of ears projected above the tall grass in a new field we'd encountered. Greyback bounded through the undergrowth, chasing them, and I followed close behind. We both stopped and scanned around, confused, as the rabbit ducked its head down and disappeared. Soon it reemerged far from our last sighting. Greyback went airborne, leaping over a clump of dirt and tearing off after our prey.

There was no way I could keep up—I just followed the bobbing tip of his tail. Since he was much closer to the rabbit than me, he must know where it was. I heard a squeak, and for a moment thought he'd caught it, but then it appeared again, far away from either Greyback or me. It was approaching the edge of the forest, and once it crossed over we would have no hope of catching it.

The rabbit made a sharp turn, moving at a speed I never thought possible. It entered a clearing, and a small furry shape appeared right in front of it—Rudy! The rabbit gave another squeak, terrified by the sight, but it was too late to turn. It ran straight at him. Rudy froze, shocked to see the creature so close. He wasn't much bigger than it was. It sped up, bowled him right over, landed with its feet on his stomach, and launched itself into the air, bounding off into the bush.

Rudy hauled himself up, partly confused, partly embarrassed, partly angry. He stood and barked at the departing form of the rabbit, as if that would cause it to stop and come back so that we could eat it.

Still excited by the chase, Greyback and I switched to chasing each other around the field, barking and nipping at each other's haunches, expending some excess energy. Rudy eventually joined in, his little legs a blur as he tried to keep up. Finally all three of us collapsed in the midst of some scrub.

All the chasing around was fun, but we were still hungry.

CHAPTER EIGHT

A STRANGE ENCOUNTER

The next morning we continued on the trails through the woods, the road spiraling gently upwards, the sun following our shadows. We were now far from the city, and the distant snow-capped mountains we'd seen all along the way were gradually moving closer.

As we walked, I gazed up at the forest canopy over our heads. The deep-green leaves shimmered in the morning sunlight, vibrating with life. The aura of each tree flowed into every other, then joined a spectacular collection streaming into the massive greater aura that enveloped the world.

A profusion of birds sang, hopping from branch to branch and flitting through the air. Crickets chirped, frogs croaked, and the leaves of the surrounding brush rustled with the movement of small animals. Points of light danced in the Web of Life, as if searching for their place in the great expanse. Everything around us was alive.

Once again we spent much of our time hunting for food. We soon encountered another open field and I tried again for a gopher, lowering my body almost to the ground, approaching from upwind, and practicing my stealth skills.

The world seemed to stand still as I crept toward my prey, not so much as disturbing a blade of grass as I moved. My snout was almost within striking distance. I pounced forward with my jaws wide, but again the animal dove down its hole just as they clamped shut, and I spit out another mouth full of dirt. We didn't even bother trying to dig it out this time.

Once in a while we'd encounter a side road, along with vehicles and the occasional house. Sometimes we would return to the main road, hoping to pick up scraps. We hadn't seen any living humans now for days, and their presence in the Web of Life continued to fade, while the component occupied by other lifeforms grew ever stronger. In the end, most of the human sources of food we found were locked away, spoiled, or otherwise inaccessible.

As it had been for many days now, the world was eerily silent. There were no more engine noises, either on the roads or in the air—no vehicle horns blaring, no screaming sirens, not even talking or shouting—only the background sigh of the wind, the tweeting of birds, the rustling of leaves, and the burbling of the occasional stream.

Greyback was proving to be a much better hunter than me. Along the way, he caught several squirrels, and scared up and almost caught another rabbit. Even Rudy managed to sniff out a few more roots, and caught a mouse and a little bird. It was barely enough to feed him, but it was something.

My own hunting skills needed work, but I was leaner, stronger, and felt more alive than I'd ever felt before. And like the world around me, I was infused with new energy, as if I was drawing some inner power from the expanding abundance of life.

In the afternoon, the roofs of a set of houses appeared in a small green valley below us. We headed down, and I crept warily up to the door of the nearest house and sniffed. The stench of death permeated the interior. I pushed and then jumped against the door, but it wouldn't move. It didn't look like any of the roving gangs had found this place.

In the back yard was a large patch of ground with plants growing in it. I could smell food buried under the earth. It was surrounded by a fence too high for me to jump, so I dug a hole underneath. Once inside, I dug under the plants and uncovered long, thin orange, and oblong brown objects clinging to their roots.

Rudy and Greyback soon crawled in after me. Remembering the wolves from before, we kept close watch as we ate. We saw nothing, human or animal. There were similar patches behind several of the other houses. In the center of the village stood a round structure with water in it. We ate and drank our fill, then lay back and rested.

I'd hoped to find another field nearby with dead cows in it, but there were none. And though the roots helped restore my strength, they weren't enough.

We kept moving, with no particular destination, just trying to stay alive. We were on our own now; whether we lived or died depended on our own skills at finding food. We explored any houses and vehicles we found along the way, knowing they might make the difference between life and death.

The sun was sinking low in the sky when we came across a stream of unpolluted water and drank our fill. We were all still hungry, but was time to search for high ground to spend the night. We found a sheltered patch on a nearby hill and were about to settle in, when I caught the scent of roasting meat. Following it, we soon spotted a thin wisp of smoke rising just over a nearby hill.

The smell of cooking meant the presence of humans. Rudy and I were especially wary after the men we'd encountered earlier, but the irresistible scent drew us forward. The three of us crept to the top of the hill, hid behind a bush, and peered through its branches at the scene below.

There were two of them, sick like all the others, but still alive, sitting around a fire, roasting pieces of meat on sticks. Beside them lay the carcass of a pig-like animal, but it was like no other pig I'd ever seen. Curling tusks protruded from either side of its elongated snout, and tufts of coarse fur were spaced around what was left of its body.

Beyond the men was a large set of buildings and metal fences. Even from this distance I could detect the scent of wild game inside. A structure that had once blocked the opening in the center was now scattered in pieces on the ground. Above that opening was a massive wall-like object with brightly coloured pictures of a huge variety of animals.

The men at the fire were intent on the skewers of savoury meat in their hands. Hungry for the game inside, we skirted around a line of scrub that shielded the entrance from their view.

The light was beginning to fade as we crept through the debris and the yawning opening, entering the compound. We all jumped as a set of lights blinked on around the top of the fence and in the interior. It was strange to see them, when almost all other places we'd encountered had now gone dark.

Inside, the diversity of scents was incredible, many I'd never encountered before. And there were sounds to match: howling, chirping, growling, grunting. We followed a curving gravel road lined with cages containing animals. There were many I'd never seen before: some like miniature humans with long arms, swinging through trees, some like giant rats, but with large, flat tails. Every cage had a different type of animal. Some appeared to be dead, but many had somehow survived.

We all jumped again at a squealing sound that echoed from up the laneway. We scattered into the shadows, just as one of the pig-like creatures hurtled past, squealing and grunting, chased by another pair of men. The men ignored us, intent on their prey.

They disappeared around a bend and we continued on. The hunger for meat drove us forward, past a human body in some kind of uniform lying beside the road, a pool of blood around its head. We stopped in front of a cage with some small squirrel-like animals that we could eat, if we could get inside. They squeaked and pressed themselves into a far corner as we scratched at the door. It was locked, and constructed of a metal mesh we couldn't penetrate.

We heard the shouts of more humans somewhere around the next corner. Creeping forward, I poked my head around to look. On the far side of an open area, a gang of men were yelling and grunting, trying to pry open the door of one of the cages with a metal bar.

I couldn't see the animals in the cage, but I could hear them bleating loudly and crashing against the fence in a panic. The men shouted angry words and kicked at the door, which still wouldn't open. The one with the metal bar stomped over to a small structure in one corner of the space.

This structure had a wooden door, like our doors at home. The man jammed the bar into the crack between the door and the frame, and pulled. He jumped back, as the door burst open. The interior was dark, but he went inside and did something, and suddenly there was light in the room, which was full of grey metal boxes with black things sticking out of them.

The man started pulling on the black things, and a few of the lights surrounding us turned off. He yelled something at his friends. They walked over and tried to open the cage doors, but they were still locked.

The man in the small building shouted angrily, lifted his metal bar, and smashed it against the boxes, one at a time. Flashes of light lit up the room, and a few more lights outside went off. A series of loud clicks echoed through the complex, and the cage doors across from us sprang open.

Bleating again and kicking, several goat-like creatures burst out of the cage the men had been trying to open. They knocked the men aside and flew down the laneway. Shouting and grunting, the men chased them past us, all headed for the entrance.

The door of a giant cage farther away flung open, and the biggest animal I'd ever seen—grey, with huge floppy ears and a long nose that almost reached the ground, lumbered out, headed in our direction. I yelped a warning at Rudy and Greyback as I backed away.

We all cowered in the space between two cages, as the massive beast raised its head and its giant nose and bellowed. The ground around us shook as it took off after the men in a frenzy, smashing against the cages as it moved. Rudy whimpered as it kicked the wire mesh beside us, making a dent bigger than he was.

We waited until the creature had disappeared, then ventured deeper into the interior. As we crossed the wide area and into a new laneway, a crackling sound echoed from the building with the grey boxes. There was the scent of something burning, and flames began to lick around its walls. As we passed by the cages, animals began screaming and howling, smashing against the still locked doors.

We kept moving. We'd just turned a corner when there was a loud bang behind us. All the lights suddenly blinked out, and a siren close by began to wail. An ominous sequence of clicking sounds echoed through the entire compound, followed by the scraping of metal against metal. A sound like thunder grew louder and louder as it approached us. Soon the air was filled with panicked screeching, grunting, and roaring, and the aura above our heads was alive with interlacing ripples.

We pressed our bodies against the nearest wall as a stampede of creatures raced around the bend—goats, deer, pigs, and many others I didn't recognize. Birds, large and small, flew screeching overhead, and smaller prey animals scampered between the feet of the larger ones. We jumped forward, hoping to bite at them, but we were soon forced to back up against the cages behind us to avoid being trampled.

There was finally a break in the thundering charge, and Greyback and Rudy took off after them. I was about to follow, when I spotted a small, squirrel-like animal that had lagged behind. I crept forward, stalking it. It got confused, heading back the way it had come and disappearing around a corner.

I chased after it, but as I entered a new laneway I suddenly froze.

I was face-to-face with a gigantic cat, many times my size, vertical stripes encircling its heavily muscled body. It had claws as big as my dog dish. It lifted its head and snarled, revealing a massive set of fangs. I turned and ran. It was so close behind I could feel its hot breath on my tail.

I dove into a narrow gap between two cages, and pressed my body against the back wall. The cat stretched out a massive paw armed with deadly-sharp claws toward me, drawing deep trenches in the ground a hair's width from my foot. The beast roared in frustration as its huge, face filled the entire opening, drool dripping from its open jaws.

The giant cat turned, distracted by a bleating sound in the direction of the entrance. It forgot about me, and took off down the laneway. I crept to the opening and peered out. One of the goat-creatures, with a man chasing it, had doubled back on the road. The cat bounded toward it and pounced, but the creature jumped out of the way and flew around a bend and out of sight.

That left the man who'd been in pursuit. He screamed at the sight of the huge beast and started running in the direction the goat had taken. The cat, which probably hadn't eaten in many days, was on him before he reached the corner. I took off the other way, toward the entrance. Behind me, I could hear the man screaming as the giant cat tore him apart.

The lights had now all gone out, but it still wasn't quite dark. Beyond the front entrance, a scene was unfolding that was unlike anything I'd ever experienced before. The host of escaping animals, of every shape and size, including several of the gigantic grey ones with long noses, were fanning out over the countryside, trampling everything in their path.

The men who had been roasting the pig lay by their extinguished fire, trampled to death. Huge birds with naked pink heads were already fighting with the crows and smaller animals to get at their bodies. Farther on, the other men who had been chasing the animals lay unmoving on the ground.

Soon Rudy and Greyback joined me. The roasted meat the men had been eating lay in the still smoking ashes of the fire. We ran at the crowd of birds surrounding it, and they exploded into the sky. They continued to squawk, dive, and harass us as we scavenged as much meat as we could. When the large pink-headed birds began to dive at us with their claws extended, we each tore off the biggest chunk we could carry, and ran for safety.

In the distance, a bizarre silhouette was set out against the reddening sky, as a bewildering assortment of strange animals thundered into the sunset, a cloud of dust surrounding them, a swirling storm of colours twisting above their heads and melding into the Web of Life.

CHAPTER NINE

REUNION

With chunks of meat from the strange pig still clamped in our teeth, we headed for the hiding place we'd picked out earlier. On our way, we occasionally saw more strange-looking creatures: a giant bird that ran on two legs, a deer with two straight horns projecting from its head, one of the pigs with big curly tusks. A group of the small, human-like creatures had climbed nearby trees, and screamed at us as we passed by.

That night I had a dream—of a time far in the distant past. I was in a vehicle with Jerry and Melanie, following the path of the setting sun. There were images of crowded roadways and frightening speeds, then of swaths of ancient forest and impossibly tall, white-capped mountains, all bathed in a deluge of unfamiliar scents.

Later, the forest and mountain images fell away, replaced by those of a dusty open plain. Eventually, we climbed a hill, and gazed out at an endless body of water that reeked of the wild world. Here the Web of Life was palpable, so thick that its components seemed to swirl around each other like colours around the setting sun. I had never felt its presence so strongly. Even Melanie seemed to have some sense of it, though her recognition was only fleeting.

In my dream, I watched in wonder as grey and white birds sailed through the air, screeching, and I dove through the crashing waves as Jerry and Melanie threw sticks for me. I remembered the sensation of my feet sinking into the sand, and of the salty, fishy scents that permeated the world.

Far out in the ocean, a gigantic fish, far larger than me, leapt out of the water and dove back in with a huge splash. I had a sense that this was where I belonged—that I was home. It was one of the most wonderful experiences of my life.

I woke, convinced now of the path I had unknowingly been following all along—the one we *should* follow—toward the setting sun to the sea, where the breezes would cleanse the air, where there would be plenty of fish and game. A place where we could make a home and begin a new life.

The next morning, fully fed for the first time in many days, we lay around our sleeping area for a while. I headed out, with a new sense of purpose. Greyback and Rudy followed. I was so full from the night before, I didn't even bother keeping an eye out for prey, as I followed a path that kept the rising sun behind us.

We continued in that direction for several days. We saw very little prey, and our bellies had long since emptied since our big meal. Greyback managed to catch a few gophers, and Rudy sniffed out a few more edible roots. I almost caught my first gopher, but again I got a mouthful of dirt—failure seemed to be stalking me. We were staying alive, but just barely. I knew I had to become a better hunter if we were going to survive.

We made our way back up to the big wide road. On the way, we saw a few other larger animals, but they avoided us, just as we avoided them. We also saw the occasional wrecked vehicle, almost always with a body inside, but other than that we hadn't seen any humans, living or dead, for days. We were walking past a dense section of forest when the scrub at one side of the road rustled. I wasn't sure whether it was the wind, or...

I stopped, and the others stopped beside me. I raised my nose and sniffed the air. Something was there. I'd smelled it before, but it was woven in with the surrounding odours; I couldn't be sure when or where. Rudy moved to cower behind me. All was silent as I analyzed the scent. Some of the tiny human-like creatures appeared in the trees nearby. They began crying out, agitated. I checked their scent—it wasn't the one I was trying to place.

Suddenly I recognized it, and I turned and started running. I glanced back as the brush parted and the head of one of the gigantic striped cats emerged. It leapt out and bounded toward us, its glistening fangs bared. I and the others were running flat out, but it was quickly catching up.

It was like a replay of my time in the city. Greyback easily overtook me, but little Rudy was falling behind. I glanced back again. The giant cat was about to pounce. I stopped and ran back to defend Rudy, stretching to my maximum height, growling and baring my own teeth.

The cat pounced at both of us, its jaws opened wide and teeth glinting in the sun. Those teeth were about to clamp down on Rudy when a deafening explosion echoed through the air. The cat stopped, startled, and looked up. A man was standing on the road behind it, with a metal stick in his hand. He raised it up to his shoulder and there was another explosion. The cat wasn't hit, but it was frightened. It ran off and disappeared into the woods.

The man lowered the metal stick and approached. We cowered and got ready to run, but his body language wasn't aggressive. As he moved closer, I picked up his scent, and I couldn't believe my senses.

"Tucker?" His voice sounded familiar, though thinner and weaker. I turned and sniffed to confirm his scent—it was Granger, Jerry's good friend from the office in town. He was unsteady on his feet, and had the same welts and pallor I'd seen on the others, but he was alive.

A large group of people, men and women I'd never seen before, slowly emerged from the trees. We all backed away, afraid. Granger made some reassuring sounds, and his facial expressions were friendly. He approached, bent down, and presented his hand for me to sniff, and

I was convinced. I rushed to him and he stroked my back as I nuzzled against his leg, my tail wagging.

He said something consoling and nodded at Rudy and Greyback. At first they were wary, but they finally stepped forward to join us. From their scents, movements, and facial expressions, it was clear that though the people in the group were sick, and probably dying like all the others, they had no bad intentions. Their only interest was in staying alive and helping each other. Unlike the ones we'd encountered earlier, they didn't seem inclined to make us part of their dinner.

Granger and the others began walking along the road. They were going in our direction, so I decided to join them, at least for a time. They could provide protection, and we could help them by detecting the scent of predators (like the giant cat we'd just encountered) or other humans who might want to attack.

We hiked along the road for several days, heading slowly toward the mountains. Granger appeared to be the Alpha of the group. I'd always liked him when he'd spent time at Jerry's. I felt safe in his presence. He seemed to have some destination in mind, though I had no idea what it was.

Some of the people died on the way. The survivors covered the bodies with brush and rocks, and we moved on. The massive rent in the human component of the Web of Life continued to expand, though much more slowly now, since I guess most of humanity were already gone.

We spotted a hill with a circular outcropping of rocks at the top. Granger, myself, and a few others climbed up to investigate. The rock formation had an open area inside that was more than large enough for everyone in the group. It was an ideal location to settle in, at least for now. It offered a clear view of the surrounding countryside, and the rock outcropping hid the interior from the outside world. I sniffed around the site, and didn't find anything bad.

Granger gathered the rest of the group, and it looked like they were making plans for a semi-permanent camp. After all the death and horror we'd witnessed since the catastrophe struck, there was finally room for hope that we might survive after all.

CHAPTER TEN

THE OTHERS

We stayed at the camp for several days. In that time, a few more people died. One day Granger took Greyback and me along as he went hunting with a metal stick. I sniffed out a deer, and Granger killed it. He and several others dragged it back to the camp. That night, they lit a big fire and cooked it. They even set aside some meat for us. For the first time in days our bellies would be full.

That night, after we'd eaten, Granger called me over to where he was sitting beside the fire. He reached his hands under my chin, and said some solemn words as he removed the article I'd been wearing for as long as I could remember—the collar around my neck. He called Greyback and Rudy over, and performed the same ceremony. Our old lives had truly come to an end.

From their interactions, I could see that some of the survivors wanted to stay at the camp forever. They were all sick, and their scents and fading auras told me that they wouldn't last much longer.

Greyback and Rudy would have been happy to stay as well. It was safer with the humans, and we were more likely to get regular meals.

But I wanted to move on. Whatever help we got from Granger's people would be temporary, and I found the mysterious call to the ocean too strong to resist. If my friends were determined to remain here, we would have to part ways.

I was glad when Granger talked to the others, and it looked like they had decided we should continue our journey. We left early in the morning, and walked until the sun was halfway up, as a few found it hard to keep pace.

Granger pointed to the top of a hill ahead of us, and nodded at the others. We climbed it, and stopped for a rest. The fur on the back of my neck rose when I caught the scent of smoke, and of another set of humans nearby. Moving closer to the edge, I saw them seated around a campfire in a clearing below us.

Granger noticed them too. I think he wanted to move on before they spotted us, but it was too late. One of them, an old man with a grey beard, pointed up at us, and the others turned to look. The old man waved, rose, and made his way to our position.

Granger's body tensed as he watched the man approach. He turned and talked to those in his group with metal sticks slung around their shoulders. They nervously put their hands on them and waited.

The old man arrived, and smiled at Granger. My hackles rose again the moment I saw him. Every aspect of his face, body, and especially his scent, screamed danger and death. But the words he spoke must somehow have convinced Granger. He relaxed and gestured to the others.

I hung back, and growled at the newcomer. I was trying to warn Granger, but he didn't understand. The old man turned to face me, and his icy stare erased any doubt. I knew we should run. But incredibly, when he turned and started walking down the hill toward his camp, Granger and the rest of his group followed.

To me, and any of my brothers, scent and body language are everything—they directly communicate an animal's, or human's, intent, and they are almost impossible to fake. But because of their difficulty reading each other's emotions, humans seem to place all their trust in the sounds each other make, even when they conflict with all the more important cues. That flaw can make them blind to the real emotions and motives of those around them.

In this life-or-death situation it was essential to understand the intent of anyone we met. So I had a bad premonition as we followed the old man and approached the crowd, larger than ours, sitting around a fire. Like all the humans I'd met, they had the sickness.

Several of the new group stood up as we arrived, and I had the same sensation of conflict between sounds and true language as Granger and his people exchanged words with them. Granger's expression indicated that he thought they were friendly, but their scents and movements showed a different agenda.

Greyback, Rudy and I hesitated at the edge of the clearing and looked at each other. We were poised to either fight or run, frightened of what was about to unfold.

I noticed that no one in this new camp had the metal sticks, unlike Granger and a few of his friends. Occasionally, when none of Granger's people were watching, the old man's eyes would dart to the sticks, which were clearly a source of power for whoever carried them.

The old man gestured toward the fire and invited Granger and the others to sit, and the two groups spent some time talking, even laughing. The old man passed a bottle to Granger and his friends, and Granger's people seemed to relax even more.

As I'd feared, the talking was having a hypnotic effect on Granger and the others. His movements became more and more relaxed. He nodded at some of his people and they seemed to relax also. They loosened their grips on their metal sticks, and finally laid them on the ground beside them.

The old man gave a subtle nod to the men sitting closest to the metal sticks, and they gradually shifted to within an arm's reach. Granger and the others didn't seem to notice. Greyback, Rudy and I watched it unfolding, but could do nothing.

I detected a new scent in the trees surrounding the camp, glanced over, and saw several people hidden in the brush. Something was terribly wrong. I had to act. I got to my feet and again growled at the old man. He turned and smiled at me, but I could sense the malevolence behind his stare. I tensed, ready to attack.

He nodded at a man sitting near me.

The man moved forward and grabbed me by the fur of my neck. I strained against his grip as I continued to snarl, my teeth bared. Granger stared at me wide-eyed. Greyback and Rudy jumped to their feet, also growling. The man holding me picked up a thick branch, and was about to club me with it, when Granger jumped up and shouted something at him.

At a nod from the old man, his people closest to each of the metal sticks grabbed them, and jumped back, now pointing them at Granger's group. The people from the trees emerged, clubs in their hands. Granger finally seemed to waken from his spell. He and a few others turned to fight, but it was too late. All the metal sticks were now in the hands of the old man's group.

I twisted out of my captor's grip, and flew at the old man's throat. He put his hands out and grabbed me around the neck. He was incredibly strong, and held me back as I tried to bite him. He stood, lifted my body over his head, and hurled me into a patch of brush at the edge of the woods.

I landed in a soft clump of grass, stunned for a moment. When I recovered and jumped to my feet, the old man was pointing a metal stick in my direction. There was an explosion, and a puff of dust rose from the earth beside me. I dove into the surrounding trees.

I crept to the top of a rise and watched from behind a wall of long grass. Granger was now shouting at the old man. He rushed toward one of the men carrying a stolen metal stick. There was another explosion, and Granger toppled to the ground, blood seeping into his shirt.

Greyback and Rudy appeared beside me. There was nothing more for us here. We ran away and didn't look back.

CHAPTER ELEVEN

RED

We ran deep into the forest, until we were far enough away to be safe. I was still bruised and bleeding after my fight with the old man. I rested for a while, then we continued along the trail. We were all in a daze, still processing what had happened to Granger and the others. I felt bad, but I knew there was nothing we could do.

I tried to put the incident out of my mind. Both groups were dying of the sickness, and would probably be gone in a few days, but that didn't erase the sadness and pain of losing my friend.

My drive to reach the ocean hadn't diminished, and there were no prey nearby, so we just kept moving. Focusing on the journey helped distract us from the horror we'd just witnessed. Though we'd all shared in the deer Granger had killed a few days ago, since then we'd had almost nothing. Now the sun was moving lower in the sky, and our bellies were beginning to complain. My ears pricked up as we entered a wide open field, and once again I heard a shuffling sound in the grass. We all stopped and sniffed the air.

They were here, I could smell them.

We arrived, and a dust cloud exploded nearby as several tan balls of fur scampered through the undergrowth. They were everywhere. Greyback and I, and even little Rudy, took off after them. We were certain they were ours, when suddenly another group of dogs appeared in the distance, chasing the same prey.

Ignoring the newcomers I dove after the fattest, slowest gopher, its scent overpowering as my snout drew near. I was about to snap my jaws on it when it put on a burst of speed and disappeared in the tall grass.

I tore after it, and soon spotted it not more than my body's-length away. It was tiring, and had paused to rest. Soon it would be mine—my success as a hunter was finally guaranteed. Again I crept within striking distance, ready to make the kill. I slunk forward and pounced, opening my jaws around its body. Just as I snapped them shut, a sudden jolt pushed me aside. Something had smashed against my shoulder, and I bit down on nothing but air.

I'd been knocked away from my prize by another dog, a reddish-brown female, who was now pursuing it. Angry, I flew after her, shoving her aside just as she was about to strike. She turned and nipped at my shoulder. I ignored her, continuing after the gopher. She chased after me, no longer interested in the prey, snapping at my haunches.

I finally stopped and turned to confront her, growling and baring my teeth. I was much bigger and stronger—she relented and backed away, growling. I turned to look for the gopher, and just caught a glimpse as it dove into a nearby hole and disappeared forever. I turned back, but the female too had disappeared. Lucky for her.

Rejoining my friends, I found that not only had Greyback caught a gopher, but Rudy had as well. I followed sheepishly as they carried their catches into the tall grass. I knew they would willingly share with me.

We had just finished devouring our kills when we caught the scent of the other pack of dogs approaching. As they came within sight, we formed a line and growled at them. One of them was Red, what I'd named the female who'd cheated me out of my prey. I stared her down, snarling, with my ears laid back, and pawing at the ground. She backed up, growling herself, but wary of me.

The new group had four members: in addition to Red, there was a male about my size but thin, with short hair, long spindly legs and a very long snout, a medium-sized female with curly yellow fur, and finally a big, dark grey, muscular dog with a large head, who was apparently their leader. Apart from the leader, all of them wore collars.

It was clear that they had also devoured their kills. Except for Red, their body language wasn't aggressive—they were just curious. We gathered and sniffed each other. Red moved forward to sniff me, but I growled, nipped at her, and drove her away. They all looked well-fed. They must have picked up hunting skills faster than us—or maybe one of them had already done some hunting in the time before everything changed.

Since there were plenty of prey in the field, and the new group didn't seem like a threat, the three of us decided to stay for at least one more day. But by now the sun was moving past the tops of the trees, and for the moment our bellies were all full. It was time to look for a place to spend the night.

When Greyback, Rudy, and I headed out, the others followed. It seemed we were a pack now, and I came up with names for the newcomers. I called the thin male with the long snout and a serene expression *Slim*. The female with curly yellow fur I named *Ginger*, because she reminded me of one of that name who used to come to the dog park. I called the big, squarish dog leading them *Block*, because of his large head.

We may be a pack, but it wasn't clear who would now be Alpha. I knew I was considered the leader of our original little group. If we stayed together, there may come a time when either Block would have to accept me as Alpha of the expanded pack, I would accept him, or we would be forced to battle it out. For now, our two groups were just traveling together. We soon found a well-concealed open space on a hill with good visibility, and lay down for the night.

The next day when we gathered again in the field, Greyback was missing. He'd been taking short trips into the forest for a few days now; I assumed that this was just another one of those, and that he would return soon.

There seemed to be far fewer gophers than the day before. Either they had moved to another location, or could smell us and were hiding in their holes. A few of us made kills (though not me), but not enough to sustain us long term. I was still annoyed that Red had cheated me out of my first kill. In the afternoon we decided to move on.

Still uneasy after the incident with Granger and the others, I avoided the wide road and headed into the woods. Block growled and glared at me as the rest followed, but he finally joined us. We soon found a trail that I guess the wild animals used to travel around. Of course, that meant that we might encounter those wild animals, but at the moment, they seemed less dangerous than the humans we might come across on the road.

In the forest, it was dark and cool. We were surrounded by a multitude of exotic smells, some familiar, some completely new. As we traveled, I began to detect the damp scents associated with water, and soon heard a deep roaring sound, and the churning of a running stream.

The air around us cooled even more as the path opened up onto a sheltered glade with a pool at its center. A waterfall, partly shrouded by clouds of swirling mist, plunged into the pool's far end. We stopped for a well-needed drink.

Ginger, the curly-haired female, drank her fill, then dove right into the pool and started swimming. Several of the others followed, and soon we were all paddling around, climbing onto the grassy bank and jumping back in. Even Red and I forgot our differences for a time, alternately splashing around, climbing out onto the shore and lying in the patches of sunlight.

At one point little Rudy hauled himself from the pool and ran up an easy slope on the far side, to a bank about half the height of the waterfall. A narrow trough, with a trickle of water, split the center of the bank and ran right down to the pool.

Ginger followed him and the two soon began sparring, nipping at each other and rolling around on the grass. Rudy climbed playfully onto Ginger's wet back, but slipped off, and bounced into the trough. Frantically clawing at the earth around the top, he lost his grip and slid down the slippery grass, landing with a splash in the water.

Ginger was watching, and followed, diving into the grassy trough and barking as she half-slid, half-tumbled down, becoming airborne for a moment before plunging into the pool. We all took turns and barked encouragement, making repeated trips to the slide and splashing into the water.

Later, Ginger plunged her snout into the rushing spray of a shallow section of the stream and shook it violently. She soon emerged with a large silvery fish, and all of us had a bite.

With a little play time behind us and a little food in our bellies, we lay drying ourselves in the sun, and watched it sail across the sky.

CHAPTER TWELVE

THE HUNT

The sun was beginning its descent when we resumed our journey along the trail. Occasionally, I would catch Red giving me a nasty glance, but she stayed well away, with the other newcomers.

We all froze when something big crashed through the trees some distance ahead. As we cowered in a nearby clump of brush, the sound moved closer, and a huge, brown animal with thick, coarse fur lumbered through the undergrowth, a pair of young at its heels. We all pressed our bodies into the earth as the massive creature stopped, raised its head, and sniffed the air. Finally it lowered its head again, and we relaxed as it continued on its way, its babies in tow.

Once we were sure the creature was gone, we continued along our original path, still moving ever upward. Usually we walked in shadow, the dappled canopy of the forest overhead. Once in a while we would break out into the open, and the spectacular white-tipped peaks of the mountains would appear, larger with every sighting.

Ginger was proving to be a skilled hunter. She caught one of the pigeon-like birds I'd missed before, and a pair of squirrels, and shared them with the rest of the pack. They would keep us all going until we (especially me) could refine our own skills. I tried for another bird myself, but it heard me coming and shot up into the trees.

We emerged from the woods and stepped into another broad meadow. Not long after we arrived, the green shoots ahead of me rustled, and a brown shape scurried into a nearby gopher hole. We fanned out, sniffing the air, watching for prey.

As I peered through the clumps of grass, I caught a glimpse of tan fur. I crept closer, and saw a part of a pink round ear, and a twitching nose sniffing the air. Soon, a nice fat gopher came trundling over the mossy ground. It hadn't yet spotted me. I crept toward it, one foot at a time, concealed behind a clump of long blades. This might finally be my chance to make my first kill.

I was within striking distance when a puff of wind licked across the field. The gopher stood for a moment, again sniffing the air. It turned and saw me, and started running. I jumped up and took off after it. Not far away, I could see its burrow. My snout was almost touching it, but the gopher was only a few of its body-lengths from escape. It looked like I would fail yet again.

A reddish-brown shape flew into my field of vision, headed for the gopher—Red, once again out to steal my prey. Angry, I snarled at her. She approached the gopher as before, and I was ready to attack if she tried to rob me of my prize.

Unexpectedly, she changed direction, circling around behind the animal, taking up a position between it and its hole. It spotted her and jumped, now trapped between the two of us. In desperation it turned to the side, but I was close enough now.

I leapt forward, and again felt an ancient stirring—a call from some deep, unknown part of my being—an urge to attack, to ravage, to kill. I clamped my jaws around the creature's body, shook it violently to snap its neck, and felt its bones crack as my teeth sunk into its fur and flesh. A deluge of emotion that was part thrill and part sadness coursed through my own body, as I sensed its essence departing from this world, and imagined a tiny disturbance, a flickering, in the vast Web of Life.

I stood triumphantly with the dead gopher in my teeth and scanned the field, intending to share it with Rudy, but I couldn't see him anywhere. I turned and saw Red standing near the gopher's burrow, her head cocked to one side, looking at me. Reluctantly, I carried my prize over and dumped it at her feet, and we shared in my first kill.

Later, I spotted another gopher and Red and I were able to successfully repeat the tactic, then once more, with Red on the attack and me blocking the escape. Again we shared in the spoils, and ate our fill.

The next day there were still plenty of prey in the meadow, so we again spent the morning hunting. Red and I repeated our team maneuver, and snagged enough prey not only for ourselves, but for Rudy as well.

We were all gradually honing our skills, and I became familiar with the hunting styles of everyone in the pack. Ginger continued to stand out as the best hunter. She wasn't quite as fast as Greyback, the speediest of all of us, but she was smaller, and could turn almost instantly. And she seemed to have an instinctive ability to track, sneak up on, and dispatch her prey.

Slim had a strange and unique style. He would stand motionless, like a spindly frame, and wait for a gopher or rabbit to approach. His body would remain so still that often they wouldn't realize he was there, or they'd mistake him for a tree or a bush.

At some point, that only Slim knew, the prey would be within his striking range. He would explode toward them, his long legs splaying ahead and behind. Over a distance, the prey would out-last him, but in short bursts they were no match. His method worked surprisingly well.

With Block's size, stealth wasn't an option, but he did have brute strength on his side. If a gopher dove into its hole to escape, he would jam his massive jaws into the dirt, and often come up with one in his teeth before it could crawl out of range. His method was crude, but successful.

Rudy's body was not designed for hunting. His snout was too flat to easily grab the prey, and he was too small to catch anything bigger than a squirrel or a gopher. His short, stubby legs were fine for walking, but his top speed wasn't fast enough to catch most prey animals. He also had trouble clearing the fallen branches, lumps of earth, and rocks we encountered while chasing through the fields.

Anyway, he never really got the whole idea of hunting. Instead of pursuing a gopher, he would often sit and bark at it. How (or whether) he expected to catch one that way I could never understand, though occasionally he unintentionally drove one toward one of us. Rudy did have one big advantage—his size. Often his entire body would be obscured by the tall grass. Occasionally an unfortunate gopher wouldn't realize Rudy was there, accidentally bump into him, and seal its fate.

Working with Red, I'd finally had some hunting success. But I was determined to master the techniques on my own. While she was napping after our latest kill I wandered off into the field to practice.

I'd just gotten yet another mouthful of air, when I felt a bump on my shoulder. At first I thought it was Red, but this time it turned out to be Ginger. She gave me a look, angled her head to one side, and I followed as she started walking. She stopped when we entered a part of the field thick with gopher holes, sat, and again gave me a meaningful look. I got the message—she was going to teach me to hunt.

She stood, and started to move. I again rose to follow, and she turned back and growled. I sat back down and watched. She stood for a moment, turning her head back and forth to listen, and lifting her nose to sniff the air. I listened as well, and turned in the direction she was watching. From somewhere below our feet, I heard a barely-audible scuffling sound.

She crept into a tall clump of grass not far from a gopher hole, and crouched down, perfectly still. She was frozen in that position for so long I was about to give up and leave, when a twitching nose and whiskers poked out of the hole, and an animal emerged. It moved nervously toward a nearby plant, pulled it out, and began dragging it back to its lair.

Ginger slowly flattened her body, and began to crawl, silently, her belly close to the ground, like a cat. I noticed that she was upwind of the hole. She continued forward, one silent step at a time, with infinite patience, until she'd positioned herself almost on top of her prey.

The gopher was headed for its burrow, still burdened with its prize. It finally caught her scent. It squeaked, dropped the plant, and ran for its life. But it was too late. Ginger pounced forward and struck, driving her snout into the hole, and emerging with a dead gopher.

She carried her prize to where I was sitting, and dropped it at my feet. Lesson over.

Later that day, Rudy had a rare opportunity when a gopher, running in a panic from me, inadvertently collided with him. I was happy when he managed to corner the unfortunate animal in a clump of brush. For once his instincts kicked in, and he made the kill. He was proudly hunched over his prize, when Block pushed his way in, growling and baring his teeth. Rudy stood his ground, but he was no match for the much bigger dog, who stepped forward, his hackles raised.

I was only a few body-lengths away. I rushed over and stood beside my friend, between Block and the gopher. Block snarled and charged at us, his lips curled back. Rudy jumped and moved submissively away. I wasn't in a position to challenge Block at that moment—I relented and left the kill to him. I nudged Rudy toward where Red and I had been hunting. He could share with us.

I noticed that Block never shared his own kills with the others in his group, and if he thought it was convenient, would steal from them, as he had stolen from Rudy. I could see that someday he and I were going to have a confrontation.

CHAPTER THIRTEEN

COMPLICATIONS

We napped for a while, digesting our meals. When I woke, I noticed that Greyback had returned. I had no idea where he'd gone off to, but he didn't seem to have come to any harm.

The prey in the current meadow were becoming scarce, so we continued on our journey. I was again in the lead, following the movement of the sun. As we walked, every once in a while I would be knocked aside by a forceful blow to my shoulder or my haunches. I would look back and see Block, staring at me and snarling.

As the sun began to sink in the sky we climbed to the top of a low hill, and saw a small town in the distance. Towns, if the humans were gone, could still be good places to find easy food. I turned toward it, planning to descend.

I glanced back. Block was staring at me with ears straight up and teeth bared. He let out a low growl, but the others were already following me, so again he eventually joined us. We descended, and on the way, encountered an open green field covered with short grass.

As we entered it we were surrounded by a swirling pool of conflicting scents, some made yesterday, some ancient. At a multitude of times long ago, a host of my brothers had marked this place. It reminded me of the park where I used to go with Jerry. We all stopped and investigated, our noses to the ground. The oldest scents bore traces of curiosity, pleasure, warning, greeting, sexual availability, and sometimes a hint of fear. But the older fear was usually superficial, not triggered by any specific event, just wariness.

There were also the scents of wild animals, most that I didn't recognize. The wild scents were similar to those for the dogs, but laced with an undercurrent of anxiety: the need to kill, or the fear of being killed.

Finally, there were the scents of humans, driven, in a hurry (as it seemed humans always were), amused, impatient (probably for their dogs), sometimes (though rarely) content. The most ancient human scents were healthy—their auras at that time must have still been firmly intertwined with the Web of Life.

The most recent animal scents all bore an overlay of fear—not the superficial fear of the ancient ones, but a deep dread, as if something terrible was about to happen. And the human scents bore little resemblance to the ancient ones: paralyzing fear, anxiety, desperation, and encroaching sickness.

The newer the human scents, the sicker and more detached from the aura they became. I looked up, and saw that more than one body lay in the weeds around us. Warily, we investigated. Some of the bodies were very old and decayed. Others looked as if they'd died within the past few days.

Greyback, Rudy and I avoided them as we left our own marks on several trees. I hoped that mine would register some kind of faith in the future. By the time we left the field it was too late in the day to risk exploring the town. We made our way back to the hill where we'd first stood, to stop for the night.

Early in the morning I awoke with a start, and opened my eyes. I'd been wakened by a scent, very close by. For a moment I didn't recognize it. I became aware of a weight on my haunches and I remembered. I looked over. Red was lying beside me, still asleep, her head resting on my body. At first I was annoyed. I was about to push her away and drive her off, but hesitated, then lay back down. I realized that I actually enjoyed having her near me, having her scent merge with mine.

I held still so that I wouldn't wake her, but raised my head and surveyed the plains below us. The light was just beginning to rise in the distance. The dark and light greys of the night were slowly transforming to the deep green of the trees standing out against the blue of the cloudless sky. In spite of all that had happened, maybe there was a chance that someday our pack would find a home, find happiness.

The others were still asleep on the grass behind us. I continued to scan around me, and stopped when my eye caught sight of Block not far away. He was sitting upright and motionless, like a statue, staring at us. I looked away.

Red stirred beside me, and opened her eyes dreamily. She flinched as she remembered where she was, unsure of what I would do, but she relaxed when she understood that I wasn't a threat. She lifted her head, hesitated, then laid it back down on my front paw.

We had all eaten well after the last hunt, and there was no hurry to visit the town. Greyback and Slim took off exploring. On their return, it was clear from their body language that they had discovered another field with plenty of prey. We postponed our trip to town and followed them. On the way, Red came and walked close to me, but I ignored her and moved away.

It wasn't that I didn't want her—I was just confused. Other than the occasional run-in at the dog park, I'd never had the opportunity to spend much time with females. I liked having Red near me, and I felt a sexual attraction to her. I knew it wasn't unusual for my brothers to have mates, but I'd never considered one for myself. Even after our connection on waking, I wasn't sure how I felt about her.

When we arrived at the new hunting ground, it was clear that it was perfect gopher territory. It was awash with their scents, and I could hear them scuffling amid the tall grass. I expected Red to join me like before in hunting down the prey, but when I looked for her, she was nowhere in sight.

I finally spotted her on the far side of the field. She was performing our hunting maneuver, circling around and blocking the escape of a big, fat gopher. I scanned the area some distance away. The tall grass parted, and Greyback's head popped up, heading toward her. They executed the move perfectly, and sat devouring their prize.

I ignored them, turned away, and set out to pursue my own prey instead. After all, I was a skilled hunter now. I spotted a twitching nose poking above the weeds, crawled forward, and pounced—and once again got a mouthful of dirt.

Despite Ginger's lesson before, I caught nothing that day. It felt like some kind of sign. The others allowed me to share, but I didn't approach Greyback and Red, even though I saw them corner two more gophers before we left.

That night, I nuzzled up beside Red, and she seemed to accept my presence. But the next day, Greyback was hanging around her, pushing between us at every opportunity, and trying to drive me away whenever I came near her. Red wasn't encouraging him, but wasn't rejecting him either.

Since there'd been plenty of prey at the field we'd hunted the day before, we returned, and Red and I resumed our original hunting maneuver. Several times, Greyback attacked me, pushing me away, and trying to complete the maneuver in my place.

Finally, I'd had enough. I ran at my former friend, nipping at his haunches. He turned and confronted me, while Red looked on, confused. We both reared up and slammed against one another, snarling and biting. Neither were really trying to do harm—it was a clash of wills, to establish who would dominate.

We backed up again and charged. As we smashed together, Greyback clamped his teeth around my muzzle. I don't think he'd intended to hurt me, but his bite tore open the skin near my mouth and it started to bleed. We stopped immediately, stepped back, and stared at each other.

For a time, neither of us moved. Red was still sitting some distance away, watching. We both turned and looked at her. She cocked her head, inspecting us both, then stood and walked away.

Greyback and I were both confused. Finally, he stepped forward and licked the blood off my lip. At least we still had our friendship.

CHAPTER FOURTEEN

A BATTLE

After two days of hunting, the prey were becoming scarce. The next morning, we finally made our way down the hill to the town. On the way, for the first time in many days, I studied the Web of Life that circled the world. The massive rend in the segment that human kind had once occupied was now consolidating, becoming more defined.

Here and there were tiny pinpoints indicating still living humans, but the points were so small it was impossible to tell whether they represented long-term survivors or just a final few who were sick, but hadn't yet succumbed. And the giant rend continued to be filled in with new life. Without the devastating impact of humanity, other lifeforms were not only surviving, but thriving.

Even the aura itself seemed brighter, and the tears that had scarred it for so many days were finally coalescing and smoothing out. It seemed stronger and more well-defined, its myriad swirling colours more vibrant, as if it was being re-energized by this sudden explosion of new life.

We reached the bottom of the hill and approached the town, constantly on our guard. We saw the occasional body lying in the open, sometimes already picked clean, sometimes still being consumed by some animal or bird, but otherwise, there was no sign of living humans.

Maybe there were no humans, but there were plenty of every other type of creature. All had been drawn by the odours of food from the houses, and the new understanding that there were no longer people around to drive them off. None were dangerous, or viable prey, so we ignored them.

We headed for the nearest and most prominent food smells. Tantalizing scents drifted from the first house we came to, but on arrival, we couldn't find any way in. We tried several others. All were locked. Finally, we encountered one with the front door smashed in. It brought back memories of the men with the metal sticks invading Jerry's house, what now seemed a lifetime ago.

We stood and listened at the opening. The only sounds inside were the twittering of birds and the scratching of small animals, and there was no sign of human life. The others hung back, while I approached warily, sniffing the air. I heard a crunch in the dirt behind me, and turned to look. Block had left them and moved up, shadowing me. I could see that he wanted to go first, but he was afraid.

Most of the wooden door lay in pieces on the ground. What was left of it hung from one remaining hinge. An angular patch of blackness extended into the interior. After some hesitation, I took a step forward. No one else moved, including Block. I slunk to the open door and sniffed again.

I stepped back, overcome by powerful odours of rage and blood lust. They coalesced into images—a gang, like the one from our house, shattering the door and storming inside.

The scents deeper in the interior told of violence and death, but somewhere intermingled with it all was sustenance. I willed myself forward, following the enticing scents wafting from a far corner.

Inside, there were a few small windows, but not much light. With every step the scent of food became stronger. I pushed forward into a room with a stone-like floor, and walls lined with metal machines. To my right was a door to a smaller room. That door was also smashed in, and the room's interior was cloaked in darkness. The odours of savagery and death intensified, but beyond them were others confirming that it was here that the food was stored.

I moved into the doorway. On the far wall were rows of shelves crowded with bags. It was from these that the scent of food was emanating. I froze when I looked down and saw several human bodies, both male and female, scattered in the space I would have to cross. I stepped closer, sniffing the air, and a deluge of scents wrapped around me like a choking cloud.

Again, images surfaced. First, the overpowering scent of terror as the group cowered here behind the bolted door. Then panic and desperation, as the door exploded in and the attackers invaded their sanctuary. Finally, despair, pain, and the stench of sexual violence as the gang killed the males, had sex with the terrorized females, then killed them as well.

I heard a shuffling sound behind me and turned to find Block standing in the doorway.

His hackles were raised, and he was staring at me, growling and pawing at the ground. The message was clear: as Alpha he should have the first access to the food. Until that moment I'd been willing to accept the idea that our group might not have an Alpha—that we would work together for the benefit of all. But I remembered Block's treatment of Rudy and the others in his pack. That, along with his other aggressive acts, were enough to convince me. I stood my ground, bared my fangs, and took up a fighting stance.

Block was a much bigger and more powerful dog than me. The muscles of his massive chest rippled as he prepared to spring forward. I watched for the telling movement, and when it arrived, jumped out of the way just in time. His open jaws, ready to clamp down around my throat, snapped together as they brushed my fur. As he passed by, I bit into his haunches. He yelped and pulled free, stepping back and preparing for another assault.

The confined room would work in Block's favour. I backed up to the doorway, then took off, heading outside. He chased after me, barking and growling, his mouth slavering. The others were still there, waiting to enter. They moved back and gathered to watch as our battle continued.

Grasping the situation, Greyback flew toward Block, his teeth bared. I intercepted him and snarled, driving him back—this was a battle I would have to fight alone. Once again Block leapt at me. I twisted away before he could sink his teeth in, but the impact knocked me off my feet and took my breath away.

I recovered quickly and we circled each other. So far, I had avoided the worst of his attacks, but I wasn't inflicting much damage of my own. With our difference in size Block had a huge advantage. I considered assuming a submissive stance and accepting him as Alpha, but in the end, held my ground. Somehow, I had to win.

Block crouched low, snarling, his lips pulled back and fangs exposed. Again his massive chest muscles flexed, as he got ready to spring.

That was when it happened.

We all heard it at once—a plaintive yelp from behind us. Block stopped in his tracks and turned to look, and we all jumped back in shock and terror. I couldn't believe what I was seeing. A huge striped cat like I had escaped before, possibly the one that Granger had scared away, now had its teeth clamped around little Rudy's hind leg, and was dragging him away.

At first we were frozen, stunned by what we were witnessing. Finally, I recovered. I forgot about the battle with Block and flew toward the monster. Rudy was yelping pitifully and trying to tear himself away, but the cat was many times his size.

I reached the two of them. The cat glanced at me, then ignored my presence. I didn't have time to plan a strategy. I leapt onto the huge beast's back and sunk my teeth into its shoulder. It reared up on its hind legs and roared, dropping Rudy, who limped slowly away, bleeding. The cat couldn't twist its head back to reach me. It shook its body violently, trying to throw me, but I held on, my claws dug in, blood oozing from the skin where my teeth had penetrated.

Finally, the beast jumped high in the air and flipped to land on its back. I would have been crushed, but I released my grip at the last moment and my body slipped out from underneath. The impact knocked my head on the ground and I almost lost consciousness, lying helpless in a daze.

I shook my head to clear it, just in time to see a blurry mass of orange and black stripes towering over me. When my eyes finally focused, I was staring at the gleaming fangs inside the cat's open jaws. Its giant claws tore grooves in the dirt as it prepared to spring, but it suddenly stopped short and roared again in pain.

I staggered to my feet, and saw the reason I was still alive. Block's powerful jaws were clamped around the cat's hind leg, and it now turned its attention to him.

I shook off the fog, and again flew at the beast. I dug my teeth into its haunches on the other side, again drawing blood. Greyback joined me, clamping onto its shoulder. The others, emboldened by our actions, attacked as well. The massive cat hauled up its leg and slammed Block's body against the ground, forcing him to release his grip, but Greyback and I continued to hold on, and by now the others were all taking nips at its sides and legs. Finally the striped monster decided it had had enough. It turned and ran.

We stood and watched as it limped across the field, patches of blood on its shoulder and leg, and disappeared into a grove of trees. We gathered to assess the damage. Little Rudy was lying on the ground, bleeding heavily, the bone of his hind leg exposed, and deep puncture wounds in his chest. Red approached and licked Rudy's wounds, then sat down beside him.

My entire body was pulsing with pain, and I had some cuts, but I was able to stand and walk. I didn't have any serious injuries. Block lay on the ground, unmoving, his eyes closed. At first I thought he was dead, but he soon woke and staggered to his feet. He too was cut and bruised, but would survive.

I turned back to Rudy. The blood continued to seep from a deep bite-mark on his leg. He made a pathetic attempt to stand, but the leg wouldn't hold him, and he collapsed right away. Ginger and Red nuzzled close to him, whimpering in sympathy and licking his wounds.

We all gathered in a circle around our little friend, nuzzling and trying to comfort him, as Rudy whimpered and closed his eyes. His body shuddered. The heaving of his chest gradually slowed, then finally ceased.

CHAPTER FIFTEEN

ALPHA

For a long time we all stood, stunned, staring at our friend. Ginger and Red continued to nudge Rudy's body, as if trying to wake him, but he didn't move. Along with the others, I gazed up at the aura surrounding us. I knew that the absence of a single life wouldn't be discernible in the vast web. Still, I felt as though I could see little Rudy's joyful soul winking out for the last time.

We made our way to the top of a nearby hill. Red came forward to support me as I limped along. The hill had a commanding view of the surrounding country. There was no sign of the giant cat, or any other danger. Soon after we arrived, Block collapsed and went to sleep. None of the others were injured. Red sat down beside me, and began licking my wounds. Greyback glanced at her, hesitated, then turned away. He took up a position on the periphery keeping watch, in case the monster cat returned. Ginger and Slim headed back down to the town we'd been inspecting.

Though every muscle in my body throbbed in pain, and my vision was still foggy, I had intended to stay awake to join Greyback on look-out. But exhaustion quickly overtook me, and I was gone.

I awoke to a shuffling sound nearby. I wasn't sure how long I'd been asleep, but the light around us was beginning to fade. Ginger and Slim had returned from town, with two large bags of food. They'd already torn them open and they and the others were about to begin feasting. At some point Block had woken and joined them.

I rose shakily to my feet, and took a step toward the food. When the others noticed I was awake, they lifted their heads and stared at me. After a moments' pause, all took a deferential step back.

That is, all except Block.

He hesitated for a few moments, his huge eyes studying me. Red and Greyback growled at him as I continued to move forward. Finally, Block took a step back as well, and all assumed a submissive position, inviting me to eat first.

We remained on the hill overlooking the town for all of the next day, and the day after that. Block and I both needed time to heal and regain our strength, and Ginger and Slim were able to find some more bags of food. The next morning, we prepared to leave this place, and its horrific memories. We headed to the town one last time, to say goodbye to little Rudy, and have one last look for sustenance.

I lay down beside Rudy's motionless body, already partially con-sumed by scavengers. Rudy had been my friend, supported me, and even protected me, for all this time. Still, in the end, I'd been unable to save him. A long shadow hovered over me, and I looked up to find Slim standing before us both, his gentle eyes peering down reassuringly.

Slim lay down and placed one paw on Rudy's, and another on mine. I felt an energy flow through me, as if Rudy's essence was somehow being guided to its final resting place, while at the same time, I was being guided toward healing. The others gathered around us, and lay down beside our friend for one last time.

Once our goodbyes were finished, we continued our search of the village, and found several other open houses with food. There was no more sign of the monster cat.

On our way out of town, we came across the bodies of the gang whose scents matched the attackers from the first house. I replayed the record of their demise. The scents told of a large group of villagers emerging from behind a building as the men passed by. They over-whelmed the gang, and rage was combined with terror as the attackers themselves became the victims. The now decaying bodies at my feet had been beaten to a bloody pulp, and were barely recognizable as human.

CHAPTER SIXTEEN

THE OCEAN

We made the trek up the hillside to the big road, thinking the wide field of vision would make it easier to spot predators like the giant cat. The road continued to climb, and every day the air seemed a bit colder. The sky had been darkening ever since we set out. Soon, drops of rain began to fall. As we walked, the drizzle intensified. A stiff wind arose, and the rain became a torrent. Sheets of water blew across the pavement, and rivulets flowed off the shoulders and into the surrounding brush.

Our coats were all soaked. I thought of the yellow jacket I used to wear when I walked in the rain with Jerry. Slim, with his thin frame and short coat, was shivering as we splashed through the puddles along the open road. It was as if the world was lashing out in anger, punishing us for allowing little Rudy to die. We came upon an abandoned car, and huddled under it for a while, but the wind blew the freezing rain funneling underneath.

Soaked and shivering, we re-entered the woods, pushing through dripping foliage, our feet squishing on water-logged moss, and eventually found a dry patch under a big leafy tree, to wait out the storm.

The sun was almost overhead when the rain finally stopped. We moved back up to the road and continued on, plodding forward, trying to forget the horror of the past few days. Greyback began to hang back from the group, and as the sun sank lower in the sky, I saw him climb a nearby hill and move out of sight. He'd been spending more and more time alone, as if he was gradually being drawn into the wild forest.

The light began to fade, and we picked out a hill with a good view of the surrounding woods to stop for the night. As I walked through the group to the resting place Red and I had chosen, I passed Block, curled up in a hollow in the ground. The sinking sun cast long shadows across the landscape, and across his body, highlighting a set of ancient scars I hadn't noticed before. They were deep, running up one leg, across his shoulder, and along the side of his face. It occurred to me that the events since the catastrophe might have somehow freed him from an even more terrible fate.

In the time since our confrontation and Rudy's death, Block had completely accepted me as Alpha. He actually seemed in better spirits now, as if a weight had been lifted from his shoulders. Occasionally, he even played with the others, and he was less belligerent and more willing to share the food. His animosity toward me seemed to have disappeared. I even thought it was possible we could become friends.

After all, he did save my life.

The next morning was clear and warm, as we made our way along the big road. Red and I climbed a hill to scout the path ahead, and soon stood gazing over an endless green landscape. I felt a breeze on my fur and turned toward it. Somewhere, deep within the multitude of scents carried on the wind, was the hint of one I recognized from so long ago. I stood for a while sniffing at the air, processing it.

I studied the position of the sun to get my bearings, then nudged Red and took off. The others followed as I climbed back down and continued toward the horizon. From then on, I would continue to follow the fleeting scent of the ocean. It was very faint—I could only detect it by climbing a hill when there was a breeze in the right direction. But it was getting stronger every day.

I'm not certain that the others understood where we were going, but I was determined, and they followed without hesitation, trusting my judgment. We continued upward toward the wall of mountain peaks that lay between us and our goal. I knew we would have to cross them. And from what I remembered of my trip with Jerry and Melanie—that crossing would be difficult.

In the afternoon, Red and I found ourselves a considerable distance ahead of the others. We'd just stepped into an open field when a solid bump against my shoulder almost knocked me off my feet. I looked over to find Red running ahead of me. The bump was almost the same as the one she'd delivered when we first met, when she'd tried to steal my prize gopher.

But this time her movements weren't aggressive—it was playtime. She turned to face me, placed her front paws on the ground, and bowed, then took off at full speed, checking back, her tongue lolling from the side of her mouth, to see if I would follow. I chased after her. She was fast and she had a head start. I wasn't sure if I could catch her.

Finally, she stopped and looked back, waiting for me. I caught up and we played in the tall grass, jumping up on each other and nipping playfully at each other's ears. I knocked against her, returning her bump, then flew away, daring her to catch me.

We continued sparring until the others caught up and joined us. Before long Ginger, Slim and I were nipping and chasing each other. Even Block got in on the action, racing around the field and play-fighting with the others. All of us played until the sun began to lower in the sky.

We found a safe place to stay the night, and continued the next morning, still on the big road. The trees around us were getting smaller, and there was a distinct bite in the air. We were heading higher into the mountains. The slopes continually steepened, and open fields with plentiful prey were much less frequent. Still, there were enough squirrels, birds, and the occasional rabbit, to keep us going, and we were all becoming skilled hunters.

As we moved, I glanced back at what remained of our pack—as we *were* now a pack—a pack with a mission. We trotted along, happy just to be going somewhere. I took the lead, sniffing the ground, and scanning the surrounding woods for water, prey, and danger. Behind me, and at my side when space allowed, was Red, whom all, including me, had accepted as my mate. Her body language said that she was content, and occasionally she or I would nudge the other in a loving gesture.

Behind us was Ginger, the energetic and playful female who had become such an important part of the pack. She continued to be the most skilled hunter, and her kills had kept us alive through many days when the rest of us had fallen short.

I noticed that lately her scent had altered. I had detected that scent before, in other dogs, always females. And it was always followed by a change in body shape, then sometime later by a particular event. There was no sign of that yet, so the event must be far in the future.

After her was Slim, whose connection with the Web of Life, and to the interconnectedness of all things, was particularly strong. His inner strength and resilience had lifted our spirits in the darkest times. And Slim's nose had been invaluable, sniffing out water, roots, and prey long before the rest of us knew they were there.

Greyback hadn't been traveling with the pack since the big rainstorm. At least for the moment, his place was with the wild world. But sometimes I would catch a glimpse of him running along on a distant hill; he was still watching out for us.

Finally, there was Block, my former adversary and challenger for the Alpha position. In many ways we now shared that role, and even now he occupied the rear of the group, watching for any danger that might creep up on us from behind.

All were my friends, and all were indispensable. The sky seemed to turn dark as I thought again of Rudy, my oldest friend—my companion since the beginning—now gone forever. His loss was a hole that could never be filled.

Still, with our improving hunting skills, and the new bond between us, I had reason to hope that we survivors would find the home we'd been searching for.

CHAPTER SEVENTEEN

THE MOUNTAINS

That night Red and I stood on the hill we'd chosen as our resting place, staring up at the star-studded sky. There was a silence now that I'd never experienced before. With humanity gone, the world was such a quiet place.

I glanced up and noticed the black outline of Slim sitting on a higher hill nearby. He too was studying the sky. Red and I headed up to join him, and the three of us sat together in that silence. A white glow lit the tops of the silhouetted trees in the distance, and soon a silver curving edge of the moon followed, bathing all around in a pale wash.

This new world was not one I was used to. It was brutal, unforgiving, and without mercy or pity. Death lurked behind every shadow and tree. But now I saw that there was beauty as well, and a new kind of freedom. The noise of humanity, and the devastation of their impact: the scars in the forest where trees once grew, the gigantic pits dug in the land, the smoke, the trash, the fences, the buildings, were all beginning to fade away and crumble back into dust, to be replaced by the green of burgeoning life.

The world was becoming as it must once have been, with only the sighing of the wind, the rustling of the leaves, and the plaintive calls of the birds and animals to disturb its existence.

Slim continued to stare upward, studying the Web of Life. His eyes closed momentarily, as if he was projecting his will on that web, and on the surrounding mountains and forest. He opened his eyes again, lifted his head even higher, and began to howl. It was a melancholy sound, channeled from somewhere deep in an endless and unknown past, one I and the others had only begun to understand.

Far in the distance, his call was picked up by our wild brothers, first from one direction, then another. Soon the valley echoed with a profusion of mournful cries. The others of the pack appeared at our sides, and we all joined in, singing our sad song to this new strange world.

The images of the trip with Jerry and Melanie had faded, but the faint impressions still remained. I remembered the air turning cold, even though it was summer, as we made our way into the mountains. Jerry had even stopped and let me out to play in the snow.

So as we moved upward and I felt a chill gathering in the air, I guessed what was ahead. Since the catastrophe had begun, many days ago, the weather had been warm, even hot. We would often be panting and have to stop moving to cool off.

The sun was still bright and there were hardly any clouds. But a bitterly cold wind now constantly swirled around us, funneling through the huge grey slabs of rock that towered over our heads on either side. And above and ahead, far more gigantic snow-covered peaks thrust into the sky.

Slim, with his short coat and absence of body fat, especially suffered. As we kept moving, every day became colder. Soon we began to see patches of snow. At first we enjoyed playing in it, digging in our snouts and sliding on the flat patches. But the novelty soon wore off, as the cold and wind bit harder into our bodies.

Still we continued upward, on the winding roadway, with tangled green valleys and trees far below us, and soaring white peaks high above. We began to huddle together at night, sheltering from the wind and snow, the longer haired dogs: me, Ginger, and Greyback, who'd reappeared for a time, taking up positions on the outside, wrapped around the others.

Slim began shivering almost constantly, and we were forced to stop periodically and gather around him to warm his body. Sometimes it would snow as we walked. I knew that as long as we were moving up-hill, the temperature would continue to plummet, and at the moment there was no sign of an end to our climb.

The weather got worse as we kept moving higher. A howling wind arose, and blew the frozen sleet into our faces. Our feet sank deep into the accumulating snow with every step, and the melting snowflakes soaked our fur.

One night we huddled together, behind a meager clump of brush. As usual, the longer haired dogs sheltered around the others. Even with our combined warmth, I could feel Slim shivering at the center.

When I woke, I was shivering. It was still cold, but the wind had finally died down and the sun was just beginning to rise. I glanced around at the others. Something was different. Something was wrong. I blinked my eyes, still waking up, and I realized what it was.

The space at the center of our group was empty. Slim was missing.

The others shifted positions but didn't wake as I jumped up, scan-ning the clearing for any sign of him. There was nothing. I moved outward, sniffing the ground, pushing through the scant brush, and crossing the surrounding landscape. I soon caught Slim's scent, heading through a scattering of rocks toward a small mountain creek nearby. The others, awakened by my movement, rushed over to join me. We followed his scent along the bank, as the sun gradually rose.

Soon, it began to snow, and the breeze picked up again. Despite the cold, we pushed on, searching for our friend, all guessing why he had left the relative warmth and safety of the pack. The snow had begun to fall heavily, and the wind to howl once again, when we finally found him.

Slim was curled up in a hollow piece of ground, behind a barren rock that partially blocked the wind. He was no longer shivering. I sniffed at him to check, but there was no need. As I'd expected, his body was cold, and there was no movement or breath. The snowflakes began to accumulate on the thin coat that had failed to protect him from the cold.

Like Melanie, Jerry, Granger, so many other humans, and little Rudy before him, Slim's beautiful aura had detached from the Web of Life. I turned away, knowing that it was my decision to travel to this place that had led to his death.

CHAPTER EIGHTNTEEN

TRIBULATIONS

Spirits were the lowest they'd ever been as we trudged with our heads down through the mountain passes, continuing our journey. It was as if death was stalking us, and I felt as though somehow it was working through me. But we'd gone too far to turn back. Anyway, we no longer seemed to be ascending, and the cold had stabilized.

Two days after Slim's death, the gloom lifted a little as we finally began to descend. By the time the sun set, the snow and howling wind had eased, the air had already become warmer, and larger trees had begun to appear. We had no sooner made the decision to stop for the night when Block suddenly disappeared into the dense brush. There was a flurry of growling, smashing around in the nearby bushes, and a series of desperate honking sounds.

For a moment all was quiet. Then the bushes parted and Block emerged, carrying the lifeless body of a bird bigger than Rudy, its long neck firmly gripped in his massive jaws.

He approached us, dropped the bird at our feet, and stepped back, inviting us to eat first. I and the others moved in and began to devour the bird. After all of us had eaten, he came forward and took a few bites himself.

The next day we continued our descent, our hope building as the snow gradually disappeared and warm breezes began to swirl around us. Greyback had taken off again shortly after Slim's death. I thought I caught a glimpse of him through the trees high on a hill, but couldn't be sure. We left the road and followed a broad path through the forest. The open fields reappeared, and there was plenty of prey. For the first time since we'd entered the mountains, our bellies were full.

Our path was now steadily downward, as we continued toward the setting sun. After several days on the trail, the trees again began to fall away. The foliage shrunk, turning into short brush, and the thick green carpet under our feet was replaced with dry, hard earth.

A few days later we were facing a new challenge. It didn't look as if there would be many sources of water ahead. The land was sparsely dotted with short, coarse scrub, with very little grass in between. It looked too dry for gophers, and I wasn't sure what other prey animals we would find. The leafy green bushes that had provided us with roots and berries were gone.

The temperature also increased as we pushed on. We'd finally escaped the deadly cold, only to be plunged into equally deadly heat. The thinning vegetation meant that there weren't many places to find shade from the now blazing sun. Still I was consumed with my vision of the sea. Even here, still far from our goal, the breeze would sometimes carry a whiff of the earthy, salty scent I remembered from so long ago.

One day, as the light began to fade, Ginger suddenly took off into the brush, and soon returned with a large rabbit in her teeth. It wasn't enough to provide a proper meal for us all, but we each took a few small bites. It would keep us alive for another few days.

We traveled for a day without finding any food or water. We were becoming aggressive and angry, snapping at each other. Even Red growled when I came near her. It only got worse the next day, as the vegetation almost completely disappeared and the sun, high in the sky, began to hammer down on us. As it reached its maximum intensity, we came across an outcropping of rock that provided some shade. We lay there, panting, until it finally began to sink toward the horizon, then emerged and continued our journey.

We traveled for a long time in darkness, on constant lookout for danger, then took refuge under another rocky outcropping. The night was cool, and in the morning we found that water had gathered in several depressions in the rocks around us. We took turns licking what we could get from them, then continued on until the heat again became unbearable.

From the memories of my previous journey, I knew our destination would be well forested, cool, and blessed with abundant water. But how many more days of hardship would we have to endure before we reached that destination?

We spent several more days plodding forward, mostly at night, with no sign of game or water. We found no more rocks to collect moisture, and no more rabbits or gophers. Every day the sun would rise to hang over our heads and beat down on us mercilessly. We would be forced to stop until evening, but even as we rested there was no place to hide from the burning disc above.

Finally one day, having traveled all night, but afraid that we would die before we escaped the heat, we continued on in the daytime, willing ourselves forward, putting one foot in front of the other. Late that afternoon, exhausted, thirsty, starving, and unable to take another step, we took shelter in a tiny patch of shade under a clump of brush.

I lay rasping heavily, my mouth and tongue dry. I fell asleep, the desperate panting of the others filling the dead air around me. I had a dream, of a crystal blue lake surrounded by tall, leafy trees, with cool breezes wafting through their branches. Red was beside me. Extending into the lake was a wooden dock. We barked at each other, then flew at top speed toward the end and dove in. I could feel the icy water enveloping my body, and taste the wonderful wet coolness in my mouth.

I woke when I felt Red stir beside me, lifted my head, and looked over at her. The light was just beginning to rise. We'd slept through the entire night. I wasn't sure if we could continue. Red lay panting, like all of us, thin and emaciated, her eyes glazed over. Her scent was somehow different. Part of it was her body's response to hunger and thirst. But there was something else…

I had smelled it before, in Ginger, just before we'd entered the mountains. I stirred as I understood that it wasn't only Red herself I needed to save. With my last iota of strength I struggled, shaking, to my feet. I had to find something soon, or we would all be dead.

I paused when I heard a rustling sound above me, and looked up to find a tiny bird perched on a branch of a nearby bush. As small as it was, it might provide some desperately needed sustenance. If I caught it, I resolved that it would all go to Red—there wouldn't be enough to share. I lurched forward, hoping to sneak up on it, but it heard my clumsy, staggering steps and flitted away. My last chance was gone.

But then, I noticed another bird, in a different bush nearby, and it flew off in the same direction as the first. I watched for some time, half in a daze, as several birds alighted and flew in the same direction. It occurred to me that maybe they were going somewhere.

The rest of the pack were too sick and exhausted to rise as I stumbled off in the direction the birds had flown. I crawled to the top of a low hill, and thought I couldn't go any further, when I sniffed at the air and my ears perked up.

Water—there was only the tiniest whiff. Another bird flew in the direction the others had gone. Somehow I found the strength to climb to the top of a larger nearby hill. Not far away lay a line of dark green, and somewhere in the distance, I heard the faint trickle of water.

I dragged myself forward, and eventually entered a grove of shady trees surrounding a tiny stream, clear and cool. I hauled myself down to the edge, drank my fill, and collapsed.

I woke a little later and felt much stronger. I waded into the stream, cooling my body and reawakening my senses, and was easily able to make it back to the others. I nudged Red with my nose. At first she didn't move, and I was afraid she was dead. Finally, she lifted her head, but then put it back down.

I nudged her again. She sniffed me, then opened her eyes. She noticed my wet fur and rose shakily to her feet, as she realized that I'd found what we'd been searching for. She licked some of the moisture from my still-wet coat, and was immediately re-energized. We roused the others, who were all desperately weak and on the verge of death. But when they sniffed me, and I turned in the direction of the water, they understood.

I led the way forward, while Block stayed at the back to look out for Ginger. By the time the sun had reached its highest point, we had all made it to the shade of the overhanging trees, and the coolness of the stream. We drank, then dove in, barked, splashed each other, even lay down and rested in the precious, life-sustaining water.

CHAPTER NINENTEEN

ARRIVAL

We remained at the stream for many days. Our ordeals through the mountains and desert had taken us to the brink, and we had all been bordering on death when we'd discovered this place. But here there was water, and lots of prey. Using our hard-won hunting skills, we had no trouble putting food in our bellies. Gradually, we all built back our strength.

The time finally arrived when we were once again strong enough to travel. I guessed that we were no more than a few days away from what I hoped would be our future home. The scent of the ocean on the breeze was stronger than it had ever been, and my drive to reach it had not diminished.

Ginger's scent continued to alter, and her belly was expanding, as the day approached when she would give birth. Red's scent was changing as well. I was sure that she would also soon bear young. I wanted to reach our goal before that happened.

We set out, following a rough trail through thick forest, the massive trees towering overhead. Red and I were in the lead, then Ginger, then

Block, as usual, watching our back. I hadn't seen any sign of Greyback since we entered the desert. If he'd been following us, he would have been subjected to the same ordeal we endured. I hoped that he had somehow survived.

To our disappointment, the patch of forest I had stumbled on ended after one day's walk, and we again emerged onto a barren dry landscape. But this time, we could make out a dark line far in the distance— another forest. We reached it by the time the light began to fade. That forest turned out to be less than a day across, and was followed by another patch of desert. But the dry patches were gradually getting smaller, and the forested areas more frequent.

Several days after leaving the last patch of desert and re-entering the forest, the thick brush, crisscrossing streams, and tall leafy trees still surrounded us. The leaves of those trees were beginning to turn, as the scents on the wind confirmed that we were approaching the city—and the ocean.

Once in a while we would encounter little villages, eerily quiet, with no sign of human life. As with all the ones we'd passed through since our journey began, they were now overrun with animals. Some were my brothers, and still wore collars or harnesses. Many more were wild: racoons, skunks, squirrels, rats, and more I didn't recognize. Whenever we passed a new town, we'd do a quick check for easy food, but in almost all cases our noses told us that it had either spoiled or been eaten.

As we passed by, we spotted a group of cows grazing in a nearby field. Unlike the ones Rudy and I had found before, there was no fence around them, and they were alive and healthy. We made our way down the hill toward them. As soon as they detected our presence, they began to snort and kick up. They made some panicked noises and started to run away. We sensed that they could be prey, but didn't really know how to deal with them, so we gave up the chase.

Days went by, and still there was no sign of our destination. The others continued to follow, but we were all getting impatient; tempers were growing short. The four of us began snorting, growling, and snapping at each other. There was now a nip in the air—a sign that winter was approaching. At one point Ginger lay down and refused to continue. I snarled and nudged her shoulder, and she finally rejoined us.

One afternoon we came upon a lush glade cut by a stream that flowed into a sparkling pool. We stopped for a well-needed drink, then for the night. The next morning, when Red and I rose and made our way toward the trail, Block and Ginger sat unmoving at the sleeping place, refusing to follow. I stopped and stared back at them, waiting, but there was no response. I returned to where Block sat and nudged him with my snout. He turned on me and growled, his teeth bared.

We'd passed through a field crowded with gopher holes on our way here, and the dense forest now surrounding us would have plenty of prey. We'd seen fish in the stream, and a thick canopy of trees formed a natural shelter. It was an ideal place to rest, maybe forever.

The tragic events of the past countless days had brought down an unbearable weight on our shoulders. But I would not allow those events to crush my dream. I turned, and Red and I resumed our journey. We had no choice but to leave our friends behind.

We traveled all morning without stopping. We were both exhausted, but pushed on, certain we were about to reach our goal. I was beginning to lose hope when we climbed a steep hill, emerged from a clump of trees into the day's bright sunlight, and gazed down at the vista below. Nestled in a wide valley, just as I remembered, was the city, its silver towers gleaming in the morning sun.

My breath caught in my throat as I scanned the distance beyond them. There it was, the infinite ocean, its deep blue surface glistening with countless flickering flashes of light. It was contained closer in by curving strips of sand, but farther away, extended to the horizon forever.

There was a rustle in the trees behind us. I turned to look. Block emerged from some brush, and soon after, Ginger appeared and joined him.

After so many days, so many troubles, so many heartaches and trag-edies, we had finally arrived. The Web of Life, the radiant breath of the world, hovered over the waters like an eternal sunrise, its components swirling and glowing with newfound energy.

Beyond the most distant curve of sand, snow-tipped mountains swept into the sky. Red moved up close, her body pressing against mine. Block and Ginger moved up beside us to take in the spectacle. I thought of Rudy and Slim. They would never experience the joy of reaching this place. We would experience it for them.

When I had traveled here with Jerry and Melanie, the city had been like the one where we lived: crowded with vehicles and people, echoing with the noise of humanity, and enveloped in a thick, choking haze.

Even from a distance I could see that, just like the one we had left, it was now a changed place. The glass in some of the tall buildings was broken. Moss, vines, and even small seedlings had sprouted in the open-ings. Eagles and other raptors soared over the open windows and rooftops, hunting for prey. There was no hint of the incessant noise that I'd encountered before, and the air was fresh and clear.

We spent the night at that spot, and the next day headed down. It was tempting to avoid the city completely. Though they now appeared to be empty of humans, cities were still their territory, and if any were still alive we would be in danger. But going around the city entirely would require a huge detour that would add several days to our journey. Instead, we took a shorter detour, avoiding the center, but skirting around its edges.

The sun had risen high in the sky before we began to pass by small houses on the outskirts. As with many of the towns we'd encountered on the way, their scents told us that many had once held large quantities of food. But a lot of time had passed. The houses that were accessible had already been raided numerous times.

In the few that our noses told us still had food, it had spoiled long ago—hungry as we were, even if we could get inside we wouldn't dare to eat it. The houses were sparse at first, but they soon increased in number, then gave way to much taller buildings with lots of windows. Eventually, we walked down the center of a wide road in the midst of a cluster of massive structures that towered over us. We all gawked above our heads, marveling at the sky reflected in their glass walls.

Again, what was eerie and surreal was the silence. This gigantic monument to humanity, which had once echoed with the roar of machines, the blare of horns, the ear-piercing scream of sirens, and the footsteps of countless humans rushing to somewhere or other, was now empty, the silence broken only by the chirps of birds, croaking of frogs, and the clicking of crickets. The ancient scents of death and despair were fading, and quickly being replaced by those of new life and new hope.

As in the city I'd escaped so long ago, the streets were dotted with vehicles, now silent and covered with red dust. Occasionally we would come across a human body, badly decomposed, and usually largely consumed by scavengers and barely recognizable.

The road where we walked, once smooth, black and hard, was quickly becoming overgrown with moss, grass, and even the seedlings of trees. Gulls, eagles, and crows soared overhead. Squirrels, scooted up and down the trunks of the larger trees on either side, rats, mice, and insects scurried along the ground.

It was gratifying to see that even here, in what had once been the depths of a city, there would be plenty of prey.

CHAPTER TWENTY

A NEW CITY

Even now that we had arrived, I had no clear destination. I wanted to find a place in the outskirts of the city, in an area similar to the one where I'd lived with Jerry, but close to the ocean. Though we knew it was nearby, here in the midst of the soaring blocks of glass and concrete we could only smell the sea, and catch glimpses of it when we climbed a steep hill. I hoped we would reach our new home, and that I would somehow recognize it, sometime this day.

We entered a broad square with a giant circular object in the center. I'd seen a structure like it before back in my city, but the one I remembered had water spraying out of it. This one was dry and coated with moss, and masses of weeds now choked the interior.

We made our way around it, warily. There was no longer a threat from humans, but there were many other possible dangers. We were out in the open, in full view of any predator that might be lurking in the shadows. We stuck close together, on a constant lookout.

As we neared an opening on the far side, the air became suddenly silent. Even the tweeting of the birds and the chirping of the crickets had stopped. The only sound was the click of our claws on the hard pavement. I scanned the many black crevices in the surrounding structures, reminded of my experience in the city when I first escaped.

We'd almost reached the opening when we heard a scuffling sound that seemed to come from all sides at once. A dark shape squeezed from the blackness beneath one of the buildings. It was one of my wild brothers—a wolf, like the ones Rudy and I had encountered so long ago. As it stalked silently toward us, another emerged from behind a huge metal box on the street, and another dove from the broken window of a parked vehicle.

Soon we were surrounded by a pack. They spread out and formed a circle around us, snarling and baring their teeth. On our previous encounter, their only interest had been the dead cows in the field. Though their brothers had joined in our song as we entered the mountains so many days ago, we lived in an unforgiving world. This time, we were their prey.

They closed in, padding around us menacingly, gradually tightening the circle. Block, Red, Ginger and I formed a ring, facing outward toward the attackers.

The pack wasn't much larger in number than ours, but they were much bigger and stronger, hardened by a lifetime in the wilderness. They moved in, first snapping at us, driving us back, looking for an opening. Finally, a big one leapt at me with its jaws open, drool dripping from huge fangs.

As it rose into the air, I dove to the ground and turned onto my back, sinking my teeth into its belly from underneath. The blood oozed around my muzzle as I clamped my jaws shut. The wolf yelped in pain, twisted itself free, and backed off to lick its wounds.

Another one beside it had gotten past me and was about to attack Ginger when a grey streak flew past from out of nowhere—Greyback! He leapt onto the wolf's back and sunk his teeth into its neck, blood now spurting from the wound. He tore at the now open gash, twisting the flesh and fur. The wolf broke free and took off, with Greyback chasing it.

Block was holding his own against another wolf. They clashed and spun in a swirling ball of fur and blood, before the wolf, its shoulder torn apart, loped away.

I heard a yelp and turned to find Red being attacked by another massive wolf. She struggled to free herself as it clamped its jaw around her leg, trying to drag her away. The panicked image filled my mind of the giant cat attacking little Rudy. I charged, butting my head against its jaw. It let go of Red and turned to face me, its fangs bared, ears laid back.

We circled each other, each looking for an opening. Finally, the monster sprang. I was sure I was lost, but the beast yelped and stopped before it reached me. I glanced back to find that Red's teeth were now wrapped around its back leg.

It turned to renew its attack on her. I sprang forward and clamped my jaws around its front leg, tearing at its flesh. Now Red and I had the wolf caught between us. We both backed up as we pulled, and the wolf yelped as I heard something snap and its front leg went limp, blood oozing from the wound. It collapsed to the ground, writhing, unable to stand.

Several of the beasts had run off, apparently deciding that we were too much trouble for the effort. Only one was left—the huge Alpha of the pack. I checked on Red. She was limping, but otherwise unharmed. Greyback, Block, and I rushed toward the Alpha wolf, but before we arrived, it lunged at Ginger, its slavering jaws opened wide.

That was its final act.

Ginger exploded towards it with all the rage of a protective mother. She clamped her teeth around the beast's throat and the blood spurted everywhere as she tore a large chunk of flesh from its neck. By the time the rest of us arrived it was all over. The giant wolf whimpered and collapsed to the ground, dead.

In the end, two of the wolves were dead, and two seriously injured. The others had run away, hopefully never to return.

CHAPTER TWENTY-ONE

HOME

I cast around to check on the others, and felt a huge relief seeing that we'd all survived. Greyback was standing near one of the dead wolves. His body language was conflicted—I sensed that he somehow knew our attackers. Had he actually been part of the wolf pack? Whatever their relationship, in the end he'd sided with us.

We were all injured and exhausted. Red was sitting to one side. I joined her and licked the wound on her leg. There was a large gash, but it wasn't too deep, and wasn't bleeding very much. She stood shakily and nuzzled against me.

I scanned the square for a safe place to rest and gather our strength. We could continue our journey tomorrow. The others followed as I scouted out a raised area in one corner, with two walls at its back and a good view of the entire space. We were about to settle there when I looked up and noticed Block walking away, in our original direction of travel.

He had a pronounced limp.

I rushed up to join him, and froze. There was a huge gash in his side that I hadn't noticed before, an open wound where a wolf's claw had struck. It was bleeding heavily. I moved up and nudged Block's shoulder as he walked. He ignored me and kept moving, with a determined expression. Devastated, at last I understood. I joined him and we continued on, heading for our new home. Soon the others had gathered behind us.

There was silence as we continued our path toward the setting sun, Block leaving a trail of blood in the dust behind him. We trudged along morosely through streets and alleys, as the sun began to move lower in the sky. He was having more and more difficulty with each step, his limp becoming more and more pronounced. We climbed a low hill and gazed at the landscape below.

My heart almost stopped. A cluster of small houses, nestled among tall grass and shady trees, looked out on the incredible ocean, and the waves crashing to the shore nearby. The rays of the lowering sun shone down, illuminating the greenery and casting a golden glow on the entire scene. I don't know how I knew, but I was certain that somewhere down there we would make our new home.

Block continued to drag himself forward. At first I didn't understand where he was going. He headed for an even higher hill and climbed it, now barely able to walk. At the very top stood a tall, leafy shade tree. Block limped up to its trunk, and sat for a moment, with a serenity I'd never witnessed before. He lay down and put his head on his paws, facing the sea and the setting sun.

I moved up beside him. I tenderly licked his face, and put my own head on his paw. The nemesis who had become a friend, who had saved my life in the fight with the giant cat, and without whose strength we would not have survived.

Red joined me and pressed herself against Block's massive chest. Soon Greyback and Ginger had gathered and surrounded our friend. Block, who I sensed had never really belonged anywhere, had finally found a resting place. In the distance the Web of Life, stronger than I'd ever seen it before, swirled like a storm above the infinite ocean.

A wheezing edge entered Block's breath, and he gazed out calmly, as the arc of the reddening sun touched the water.

He was home.

CHAPTER TWENTY-TWO

A NEW WORLD

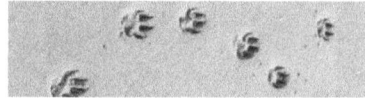

Giant glass and concrete blocks, now wildly overgrown with vines and brush, loomed over my head as I trotted along a street near the edge of the city. I scanned the surrounding buildings and sidewalks, and the underbrush that had taken root in every available corner. Danger always lurked in the shadows, and the scent of the dead gopher clamped in my teeth would tempt many hungry predators.

The wolves we'd encountered on our arrival were still around, along with an assortment of other carnivores. There were many I didn't recognize, but had ample reason to fear. I even caught a glimpse of one of the huge long-nosed animals we'd seen so long ago, lumbering down the street and into the surrounding forest. Though I'd yet to see them, I dreaded that the giant cats might also have made their way here.

As I walked, I glanced up at a nearby hill, where Block's bones still lay by the tree he'd chosen as his resting place. He was at peace now. Once in a while I would make my way up there, to pay my respects and wish his spirit well, now that it had departed from the Web of Life.

We hadn't seen a live human since we arrived, and the city was quickly reverting to its natural state. Grass, bushes, and even small saplings now sprouted from the pavement, and numerous streams had carved out paths through the low-lying areas.

Not long after we'd arrived, it had gotten cold for many days, and there had even been a sprinkling of snow, bringing back horrifying images of our ordeal in the mountains. But the cold was now receding, and the snow had melted long ago. Green shoots and blossoms were beginning to appear on the trees.

There was no shortage of prey. Many squirrels, rats, mice, and birds had established themselves inside and underneath the crumbling buildings, and in the trees lining the streets. Here and there were also plots of land that contained plants with roots that were edible, and we found some trees from which fruit sometimes dropped to the ground.

As the sun moved high in the sky above the sparkling blue waters, I passed through a wooden gate now falling from its hinges. It was part of a picket fence that was itself collapsing. I continued down an overgrown cement path to the front door of a small wooden house—the place the survivors of our pack had claimed as our territory.

One side of the structure was blackened and crumbling, and still carried the faint odour of smoke. The den Red and I had set up was on the other side, high above the broken furniture scattered around the lower floor. What had once been a set of wooden stairs leading to the den had collapsed, leaving only a narrow slope for access. Any attackers would have to move one at a time to reach us. A large section of the roof was now gone, but the part above our den was intact, providing shelter from the rain and wind.

A large hole in a nearby wall, where a window had once been, gave us a good view of the outside, and of any dangers that might come our way. We also had a view of the wide blue expanse of the ocean. We could smell the fresh sea breezes, and listen to the gulls as they soared through the smokeless skies. A small stream now ran through the house from outside, providing us with easy access to water.

Our four pups, one male and three female, had been born not long after we arrived in the city. They had now reached the active stage where they tore around the den and play-fought constantly.

Ginger had a den in the corner opposite ours. Her pups were a little older, and they acted as big brothers and sisters to ours. When they were born, only a few days after we arrived, two of the three looked a lot like Ginger. The third was considerably larger than the others, dark grey in colour, solidly built, and had a large, squarish head.

Since that time the large grey one had continued to grow and was now almost the size of his father. I thought again of Block every time I saw him. It made me happy to know that at least my friend's legacy would live on.

Greyback had left for the wilderness not long after our arrival. He had been vital in our fight against the wolves, but the wild spirit had come to dominate him, and staying in the city was no longer an option. Still, I had no doubt that we would see him again.

I entered the den, still carrying the gopher in my teeth. Red lay in her chosen corner on a large square cushion, her flame-coloured fur bathed in the light of the morning sun. She was licking one of the pups clean, as the others squirmed and whimpered next to her.

I stood for a moment admiring her, a warrior she-wolf when the circumstances demanded, but a gentle, nurturing mother now. She looked up contentedly as I dropped the gopher at her feet. I was home, in a place I'd always dreamed of, in a world so stunningly different from the old one, yet in some ways so much better.

That same day, as the sun started on its downward path, the pups bounded through the grass on a hill beside me as we headed toward the beach. Now that they were old enough, it was time to take them outside the den, and begin their education about the world. Two of them lost their footing and ended up rolling most of the way down. They were still clumsy and ungainly, still learning how to move. But soon they would be fully grown and strong, and have families of their own.

We gathered on the beach, several of them already covered with sand. They jumped and sparred with each other, growling and whimpering when their ears or tails were bitten by their siblings. They ran along the sand and into the surf, yelping occasionally as a breaker took them by surprise. They chased the seagulls, sniffed at the seaweed and the crabs crawling on the sand, and dug furiously at the tiny holes, looking for the clams buried underneath.

They had a huge advantage I'd never had when I was a puppy. They would grow up free. Their lives would be hard—finding prey, battling the elements, and fighting off enemies, but they would be in control of their fates. There would be no humans to feed them or take care of them, but they also wouldn't be forced to adapt to human ways.

The sun had moved lower in the sky by the time one or two of the pups began to flop down in the sand, slow to build up their energy again after a bout of play. Their rest periods got longer and longer, and I knew it was time to go home. I nudged them from behind as we made our way back up the hill and into the trees, heading for the den.

That's when I saw it—high up on a hill in the distance—a solitary but familiar figure. Its features were outlined by the setting sun, but it was unmistakable, walking on two legs, holding a stick in its right hand. It was too far away to be sure, and I couldn't detect its scent or its aura, but the figure appeared to be healthy. It stopped and slowly turned its face up to study the sky, staring intently at something.

What it possible that the figure was studying the Web of Life? Could the ability to see it be the key to surviving the tragedy that had struck humanity?

I gazed up myself at the fantastic aura of the world. The human component that once almost completely dominated had now all but disappeared. The void that had formed after their disappearance was now teeming with a breathtaking profusion of other lifeforms; the aura was being restored to its original balance. Still, I thought I could detect a few tiny points of familiar light, and there was no sign of the sickness in them.

The figure looked down again, and continued on. I couldn't decide whether to be happy or sad. Whatever the final outcome, I hoped that maybe things would be different this time.

AUTHOR'S REQUEST

MY KINGDOM FOR A REVIEW!

Thank you for reading Tucker vs the Apocalypse — I hope you enjoyed reading it as much as I enjoyed writing it!

I know there are millions of books out there for you to choose from, and I'm honored that you chose mine. It's a challenge for authors like myself to reach new readers, and this is where you can help.

If you enjoyed this book and think it would be of interest to other readers, please write a customer review on Amazon.com. A few words are all that's required. Positive reviews are the best way to attract new readers, and I'm grateful for each and every one I receive.

Jay Allan Storey

ABOUT THE AUTHOR

Jay Allan Storey has traveled the world, passing through many places in the news today, including Iraq, Iran, Afghanistan, and the Swat valley in Pakistan. He has worked at an amazing variety of jobs, from cab driver to land surveyor to accordion salesman to software developer.

Jay is the author of eight novels: **THE ARX**, the **BLACK HEART** series, **ELDORADO**, the **VITA AETERNA** series, and **THE HOUSEBOAT DETECTIVE**. He's also the author of a novella, **TUCKER VS. THE APOCALYPSE**, a number of short stories, and several screenplays. A new novel is currently in the works.

His stories always skirt close to the edge of believability (but hopefully never cross over). He is attracted to characters who are able to break out of their stereotypes and transform themselves.

He loves both reading and writing, both listening to and playing music, and working with animals. He's crazy for any activity relating to the water, including swimming, surfing, wind-surfing, sailing, snorkeling, and scuba diving.

Jay is married and lives in Vancouver, BC, Canada.

Contact Jay at:

Website: *www.jayallanstorey.com*
Email: *jayallanstorey@shaw.ca*
Sign up for Jay Allan Storey's mailing list at: *www.ee-purl.com/MH-Sv*

ALSO FROM JAY ALLAN STOREY

THE BLACK HEART OF THE STATION

(The first book of the stunning Black Heart series)

Delinquent or Prophet? Whichever one teenager Josh Driscoll is, he may be the Station's only hope for survival.

The Station is a city buried deep beneath the surface of a frozen, lifeless Earth, its origins lost in the mists of time. Josh's frequent rule-breaking exploits are focused on a single question — how did we get here?

But Josh goes too far when he steals a space-suit and escapes to the surface to explore.

As punishment, the governing Council, of which his father is a member, forcibly enrolls him as a novice monk at Saint Carmine's, the Station's resident monastery. At first desperate to escape, Josh finds himself drawn into the monastery's ancient texts.

Deciphering an encrypted journal hidden for centuries, Josh learns that the Black Heart, a computer complex sealed off after an ancient asteroid strike, may hold the answers he's been seeking, and may be all that can save the city from certain annihilation. When the deranged head of the Council is determined to demolish the Black Heart and doom them all, Josh leads a desperate battle to stop him.

But can Josh and his tiny band of followers prevail in time to avert catastrophe?

What Readers Say About The Black Heart of the Station:

★★★★★ 'It's a long time since I've stayed up until 2 o'clock in the morning to finish a book, but I honestly couldn't put it down.'
★★★★★ 'loved all of Storey's books so far, but this is definitely my favorite.'
★★★★★ 'This tops my favorite's list in this genre.'
★★★★★ 'I rarely give 5 Star rating but this book and author demanded it.'
★★★★★ 'One of the best I have read in a long time.'

VITA AETERNA

(Book One of the mind-bending Vita Aeterna Series)

With the fate of the world in the balance, one outlier could tip the scales towards salvation or disaster.

Alex Barret lives in 'the Quarters', a set of broken-down slums surrounding a glittering walled-off city called the First Circle. Like all kids his age, on his sixteenth birthday Alex is scheduled for Appraisal, an unpredictable medical procedure with the potential to extend his lifespan. In a world where everything else costs, for some reason Appraisal is free.

But no Appraisal scenario Alex has ever heard of has prepared him for his own experience - he's abducted, imprisoned, and subjected to brutal medical experiments in a high-tech lab. He escapes and goes on the run, a heartbeat ahead of a ruthless army led by the most powerful man in the world. Piecing together the clues behind his kidnapping, he uncovers a treacherous plot that only he can derail.

But to succeed, he must penetrate the First Circle, the forbidden abode of the ruling class.

What Readers Say About Vita Aeterna:

★★★★★ 'I absolutely loved this book.'

★★★★★ 'Never read anything quite like this, read it!'

★★★★★ 'One you have to read!'

★★★★★ 'Awesome plot. Unique! Thank you for writing it.'

★★★★★ 'An excellent dystopian novel with plenty of action.'

★★★★★ 'A must read for anyone who loves a good, original adventure/thriller!'

★★★★★ 'Get ready for amazing action and adventure!'

ELDORADO

Lost and alone in the desolate wasteland that was once Suburbia.

In an energy-starved future, Richard Hampton's world is blown apart when his younger brother Danny disappears and the police are too busy trying to keep a lid on a hungry, overcrowded city to search for him.

Richard has to make the transformation from bookish nerd to street-smart warrior to survive when he jumps the 'Food Train' for the disintegrating suburbs in a desperate search for Danny and his dog, Zonk.

Branded a criminal by a community of outcasts and condemned to death, Richard is rescued by streetwise Carrie, who joins in his search. As they trek across the remnants of suburbia, facing criminal gangs, renegade militias, and the hardships of the road, their friendship evolves into something more.

The trail finally unwinds at a deserted complex in the remotest corner of the sprawling suburbs.

The incredible secret they uncover there will alter their lives and their world forever.

What Readers Say About Eldorado:

★★★★★ 'Amazing read of an amazing futuristic journey.'

★★★★★ 'An engaging and thrilling adventure.'

★★★★★ 'On the edge of my seat throughout the whole thing.'

★★★★★ 'I was hooked right from the get go.'

★★★★★ 'Can't wait for a sequel. Very believable, couldn't put it down.'

THE ARX

Ex-Homicide Detective Frank Langer is a broken man — but he's all that stands in the way of a deadly conspiracy.

Since a mental breakdown put him on medical leave from the squad he was once hand-picked to lead, Frank spends his days drinking and chain-smoking, and his nights waking up screaming from a horrific recurring nightmare.

Until one day, by chance, he stumbles upon a monstrous plot to kidnap children.

When the mother of one of the missing children commits suicide, Frank is driven to see justice done. But when he shows up at the squad with the wild story, his former colleagues pat him on the back and tell him to go home. Instead, he stamps down his demons and, together with the dead woman's sister Rebecca, plunges into the case.

One heart-pounding step ahead of the conspirators, he races to fit together the pieces of an intricate puzzle. When he finally unravels the mystery, the answer is more deadly than he ever imagined.

But can he stay alive long enough to find someone to buy his story?

What Readers Say About The Arx:

★★★★★ 'One of the best books I've read this year.'

★★★★★ 'Recommend it from beginning to end.'

★★★★★ 'Love this book. Kept me reading & wondering where it was all going.'

★★★★★ 'One of those "can't put it down" novels we hear others talk about but rarely find ourselves.'

★★★★★ 'The Arx by Jay Allan Storey is a TOP READ.'

THE HOUSEBOAT DETECTIVE

A good detective has an analytic mind, loves to solve puzzles, is driven to know the answers - oh, and he might play piano.

Twenty-something Jake Sommers lives in a houseboat moored at Fisherman's Wharf, a picturesque set of docks bordering the Inner Harbour of Victoria, BC. Jake inherited his craft, the Honeysuckle Rose, from his late Great-aunt Dierdre, once a successful artist and sixties flower child. Jake's a bit of a lost soul, who plays piano in a bar, loves the jazz music of the 1920s and '30s, and has a tendency to drink too much.

When a beautiful woman shows up at his floating home mistakenly believing Jake is a qualified and experienced private investigator, and begging to hire him for a case, the little voice in Jake's head tells him he should turn down the offer.

Too bad he never listens to his little voice.

He expects his 'investigation' to be a straightforward search for a young woman on the Internet. But both his client and her case turn out to be far more than he bargained for, and he's unwittingly plunged into a convoluted world of DNA ancestry, danger, intrigue, and murder.